Miss Mary's Honor Guard

DONALD C. BOWMAN

For Lornee,
a Lady of the South!
one of the Unvanquished,

Don Bowman

Miss Mary's Honor Guard

Published by Wheatmark®
610 East Delano Street, Suite 104
Tucson, Arizona 85705 U.S.A.
www.wheatmark.com

International Standard Book Number: 978-1-60494-398-6
Library of Congress Control Number: 2010930438

To My Bride, whose love, talent, and courage have inspired me
for nearly fifty years. She creates beauty wherever she goes;

And to the Troopers of the First Cavalry Division of all eras, may
we all meet again on Fiddler's Green.

Introduction

The major events in this story really happened. I have taken some liberties with Morgan's first raid on Lexington. The technique of misdirection by allowing civilians and captured Union soldiers to overhear conversations about the next objective were actually used by Morgan extensively. When believed, they diluted the resistance found at the real objective and, after a time, were disbelieved even when the information was true. Morgan also used an expert telegrapher, "Lighting Ellsworth," to tap into telegraph lines and send extensive deceptive traffic to Union operators. Morgan's grand raid into Indiana and Ohio is described in detail in a number of books. *The Longest Raid of the Civil War* by Lester V. Horowitz gives the most detail about the route followed, as well as daily actions. General Basil Duke also gives a fine first-hand account. Morgan's raid by about 2,200 troopers engaged about 250,000 Union troops in pursuit and capture during the critical time of the fall of Vicksburg and the Battle of Gettysburg. It still was not enough to avert those defeats. About 700 men of the command escaped across the Ohio River to the south. The rest were captured and interned in prisoner-of-war camps. An excellent description of those camps can be found in the book *While in the Hands of the Enemy* by Charles W. Sanders, Jr. Morgan and a number of his officers were imprisoned in the Ohio Penitentiary but escaped. Morgan was later killed in battle in Greenville, Tennessee. Command of the remnant of his men fell to his brother-in-law, Basil Duke. That command, strengthened by men exchanged just before the war's end, was part of the escort for Jefferson Davis in his flight south.

In 1862, Morgan married Martha Ready, a belle of McMinnville, Tennessee. She was a popular figure in the South and the name was well known. Cynthia's assumption of the identity of a fictional niece of Mrs. Morgan was entirely believable at that time. Richard Gano's Squadron of Texas Cavalry had joined Morgan's command shortly before the wedding and committed a minor *faux pas* when they were caught stealing chickens from the Ready family hencoop. As fighters, they were more successful than they were as chicken thieves and frequently acted as the advanced guard for Morgan's command on the march. The first raid on Lexington attracted so many volunteers to Morgan that he used Gano's squadron as the nucleus of a new regiment. He designated it the Third Kentucky Cavalry. He was not aware that that designation was already in use. The regiment was later designated the Seventh Kentucky Cavalry.

All of the general officers mentioned in the book are real except Martin Hurlburt. He is entirely fictional. Generals Crook and Kelley were, indeed, captured right under the noses of their own 8,000-man army by Lieutenant McNeill and his Rangers. The real names of those who participated in the operation and the course of the operation itself are substantially as described here. A West Virginia History website gives an excellent description of the entire event, which I have abbreviated somewhat. It was an exciting tale that deserves more attention. Crook and Kelley were exchanged, and Crook commanded a Union Cavalry division in the pursuit of Lee's Army from Petersburg to Appomattox. Later, he was a renowned Indian fighter on the frontier.

LTG Richard Taylor was the son of Zachary Taylor, President of the United States. A man of fine education and courtly manners without experience as a professional soldier, he, like Forrest, rose to the rank of lieutenant general. Of his four children, only his two daughters survived a scarlet fever epidemic. Both small boys died within days of contracting the disease. His property was looted and destroyed by Union forces.

Escape and evasion of captured Confederates was not at all uncommon. H. B. McClellan, who was an aide to Confederate

General J. E. B. Stuart, was captured by Union forces and escaped. He worked for a time in the oil fields in Pennsylvania and brought his fiancée north to marry her in Philadelphia during the war. When Morgan was cut off and surrounded, the prisoners were put aboard river boats for shipment downriver to Cincinnati for rail transportation to Camp Douglas. One Confederate changed into natty civilian attire and simply walked off the boat swinging his walking stick when it docked. The incident of the black dog at Camp Douglas, Illinois, was widely written up. The story was told to me by my grandfather as though his father and uncle had been part of the plot. That and other disruptions were carried out by Morgan's men, who were rated as the worst troublemakers by the Union camp commander.

Don Bowman
Columbus, Georgia

Book One

War

Chapter 1

The Union cavalry trooper lowered the sights of his carbine from the Confederate standing in the open tending to his horse. It was not quite sunup; the light in the open meadow below him was still very poor, and the wooded ridgeline where he lay concealed was even darker. He recognized the piebald horse that he had seen several times in the last two days.

"Lieutenant, one of the Rebs from that scouting party we've been tracking is right out in front of us. He's too far away to shoot; let's catch him."

The lieutenant slipped down from his horse and ran up the hillside to join his scout, creeping the last few yards on all fours to a point where he could see the far side of the ridge. He watched the Confederate examine the right foreleg of his horse and noted that the man was only about three hundred yards from the base of his hill. The blue officer waved forward his eight men waiting below and ran for his horse followed by his scout.

"Let's get him! At a gallop! Follow me!"

The blue horsemen thundered over the ridge crest and down the hill on the main road at a full gallop. They could see the startled Confederate look up and swing into the saddle without wasting time for a shot. They closed rapidly on him as they approached his former position at a small crossroads. Fence posts flashed by as they thundered after the struggling man. Just before the lieutenant reached the crossroads, twenty-four men in gray rose from the ditch and fence along the intersecting lane and fired at him. There was a sheet of flame and a deafening roar. Gray smoke erupted from the muzzles of the rifles. The lieutenant and his horse went down, bringing down two men who were close behind him. Four others were shot out of their saddles and two horses were crippled. Pistols out, the Confederates swarmed over their fallen enemies. Only the scout who was lagging behind was able to pull up and turn back for a run for his life. His horse was wounded by a rifle shot before he made the ridge, and the Confederate mounted on the supposedly lame horse rode him down and took him prisoner.

The Confederate officer in charge of the ambush party, Lieutenant John McKenzie, waved to the ridge farther south, and five troopers leading the party's horses brought them forward at a lope. His sergeant reported four Union soldiers killed, two wounded severely, and two badly injured. Two were captured whole. Five Union horses were serviceable. The other five were destroyed. The men had already salvaged any usable arms and equipment.

"Them people never fought Comanches," the sergeant remarked as he spat philosophically after giving his report.

"No, nor if they did, did they learn anything. We would never have been able to shake them. We have to move very fast to be in Cranmer in time for our meeting this morning. Pick two men to take the prisoners back to General Morgan. He should be about ten miles southwest of here. We will pick our boys up tonight after this job is over."

The two gray riders pierced the forest shadows and arrowed along the road from the southeast into Cranmer. As they neared the edge of town, one went ahead of the other. Reins were held high in front of their bodies and the Enfield rifles that they carried were leveled and ready. The tension in their bodies warned of a lightning reaction to any threat. They were mindful of the carnage they had visited on their enemies a few hours ago and were determined to prevent the same thing from happening to them.

Ed and the few townspeople who were on the street at this early hour stared silently at them as they advanced. No one knew what this meant, and the arrival of armed men brought tension to the civilians to match that of the riders. The lead rider scanned each face, catching the eyes of men and women alike, until he rode past. The second rider did the same, but he smiled as he caught their eyes. At the fork for the bridge over the river, the first rider turned and rode across the bridge, while the second sat his horse at the intersection of the three roads. He faced the eastern road after his partner rode out the western branch.

In a minute, the first trooper was back to the intersection and past his companion. At a trot, he rode to the edge of town along the road from the southeast and waved. Ed could see about twenty-five riders in a column of twos come out of the forest verge at a gallop. The unison of their movement and their tight formation meant power and aggression. He was spellbound, silently watching the spectacle.

At the edge of town, the officer at the head of the column signaled to walk horses, and the men reined in to a walk instantly. Had it not been so martial it would have been rather pretty. The officer had the big yellow loops of braid on his sleeve that singled him out from the soldiers in his column, but his dress was very much like theirs. He wore his pants tucked into high tan boots with big spurs. Ed had never seen a spur like that except the spur that Mr. Goddard, the banker, had hung on the wall behind his desk. A Mexican spur, Mr. Goddard called it. Mr. Goddard had brought it home from the Mexican war fourteen years ago when Ed was just fifteen.

Things had been quiet in this part of Kentucky since the beginning of the war in April of 1861. Some of the boys from the village had gone off to join one army or another, but none had gotten home to tell tales of war and adventure. Of course, there had been some bushwhackers over to the east that preyed on travelers in the name of one side or the other. Nobody from the town had been hurt that Ed knew of. This was something different. This was war on his doorstep and it made him very uneasy. He didn't like that feeling at all. Should he go back inside and hide all of his valuables, or would they see that and follow him? Were they going to drag him off to the army and make him fight? He finally backed into the shadows and watched fearfully.

The alert troopers all looked both right and left as they rode into town, some smiling and nodding at the townspeople.

Ed found all of this reassuring and slipped out of the shadows and walked tentatively toward the center of town so that he could see what was going to happen, while keeping a safe distance behind the column of soldiers. He could see the troop dismount after sending a few men mounted out each road and across the bridge. Almost magically, every small boy in town appeared in front yards and on porches. The noise of the trotting horses was replaced by the sound of motherly commands to come back inside or to stay on the front porch. It was all a waste of breath for the mothers of the town. Only a very few timid souls obeyed the pleas and threats of their mothers. In five minutes, exercising the natural affinity of boys and dogs for soldiers, every trooper in the center of town had several small boys in his shadow.

The silence was broken for good now, and several voices called out, "Hurrah for Dixie!" There were a few other calls that were not so friendly, too, but those callers elected to do their calling anonymously from the concealment of their houses. They need not have worried, as they were ignored.

Before long, some good women of the town sent out pitchers of milk or fresh bread for the dusty men. In every case, the bearer was saluted with words of gratitude.

Albert Goddard stood well back from his front window and watched the officer and the sergeant closely. All of this smiling and friendliness did not reassure him at all. He could not risk going outside just yet. He had to find out what they were here for first. His firearms were all hidden away except for a small revolver that he had given to his wife when he took her upstairs and locked the door to her room.

"It is just for safety, Elizabeth. Sometimes troops are very disorderly when they come to an enemy town." He knew those spurs. He remembered the Texas Rangers who were with the army in Mexico and shuddered at the thought of what they might do to him as a strong Union man.

Yes, he had to admit it. He was afraid of them for himself, not for Elizabeth. She was partial to secession, really. It was that old beau of hers, Homer Montgomery, who was off somewhere in the Rebel Army. "Damn! These couldn't be his troops, could they?" Beads of sweat came to his legs and his pulse fluttered a little. "Maybe he found out that I was the one who got some of his property in '61 when Charlie Flannery foreclosed on him after he left for the war."

Except for their officer, the soldiers in the street were relaxed with that familiar confidence that all good soldiers have. He watched the people talking to the Confederates and tried to identify the townsmen who seemed most friendly. That information might be useful later. Then he saw Ed Barton moving slowly toward the men in the street. Ed was the perfect tool to get what he wanted without risking himself. When Ed stopped in front of his house, Goddard eased up to the window and called, "Morning, Ed. What's going on?" His voice sounded strangled and quivery to his own ear. "God, help us; I hope I don't sound like that to him," he thought.

"Morning, Mr. Goddard. I don't really know. These soldiers just come riding in to town and stopped at the crossroads."

"Who are they, Ed. Do you know? I don't like soldiers coming into our town and upsetting the good people we have here. What do they want? Whose men are they? Why are they here instead of somewhere else? We need to find out for the good of the community, I think. Don't you? Go ask them! I would but I am not dressed yet. I would be obliged to you if you would do that while I dress."

Ed wondered how much Mr. Goddard would really be obliged to him. He couldn't remember Mr. Goddard acting obliged to anybody. There was a long silence while Ed turned it over in his mind.

"Ed, I need you to do what I asked right now." There was an edge in Goddard's voice that Ed had heard before. It was not a friendly tone, but the voice was at least two tones higher than Ed had ever heard it before. Ed knew his tones. He was the best fiddler in the town. Ed was not sure why Mr. Goddard's voice was getting so high, but he thought it might be better to move on down the street a bit and just watch some more before asking questions that these strangers might take offense at. Ed moved on toward the group of soldiers as reluctantly as a man going to his own hanging. He was afraid. There were too many bad things that might happen if something went wrong. The sloped shoulders turned slowly toward the troopers and the townspeople and began a few deliberate steps closer to them.

Goddard cursed and withdrew from the window to a chair where he sat hunched forward, his face frozen, intent on the scene before him outside.

The officer and the sergeant had remained in the center of the intersection, so only a few townspeople were close to them. The lieutenant reached for his watch again. There was a flash and a ping as the cover sprang open. He bent his head to it, then turned and scanned the sky, fixing on the height of the sun by twisting to the east. "It's time." Impatience and exasperation could be heard in his voice.

"All right, boys, check your cinches and equipment. Give back the baskets and linens."

Children were lifted from saddles. Mothers hurried into the press to retrieve the smallest boys, shouting at the older boys to come away. Townsmen stepped back to the edge of the street, saying little.

"Prepare to Mount! Mount! Sergeant, column of squads! Take them out!"

"Column of squads. Second, first, and third, on the north road, Forward, Ho! Out riders in!" The squads fell into a column of two mounted men abreast heading across the bridge and out the north road. The ease and humanity were gone. The group was no longer several young men in the sunshine. It was once more an integrated part of a killing machine. The outriders turned from the edge of town and rejoined the main column in their accustomed places at a fast trot. "George, attend the lieutenant!"

The smiling trooper reined his horse out of the column and trotted to a position to the left and rear of his officer, who continued to stand holding the reins of his horse in the middle of the intersection.

Mr. Goddard, emboldened by the peaceful departure of the Rebel Cavalry, stepped out onto his front porch fully dressed. He saw Ed standing with his hands in his pockets on the side of the street, the very picture of indecision, looking at the young officer. He realized that he would not find out what he wanted to know through Ed's efforts. He would file that little failure away for future use. With only two rebels left, his feeling of safety was much greater. After all, this was his town. He owned most of it or soon would, and he wanted to be in charge of everything that happened in it. He stepped down the front steps and walked easily down the street toward the intersection. As he passed Ed, he made a noise that sounded like a cough but not quite.

He touched his hat brim to the young man cordially and strode over to him. He was pleased to see the officer turn his attention from contemplation of his watch and straighten to a respectful attention. The gray uniformed man was about middle height, broad shouldered, and clean limbed. In general, he was just another well-proportioned young man with a nice but unremarkable face—except for one thing—his eyes. His eyes were dark, deep set, and large. His gaze was direct, probing, and intelligent. There was force. It gave Mr. Goddard a start, and he hesitated in mid-stride in his approach. He brought up too short to comfortably reach out and shake the man's hand; he had to take another half step to grasp the outstretched hand. He had meant to lead the conversation from the start, but he found himself responding to a friendly greeting and a firm handshake.

"I am honored to make your acquaintance, sir," the young man said respectfully. "The hospitality of your citizens has been most generous and gratifying during our short stay."

"Ah, yes, Captain! Too short! Too short! Must you continue on far today? I had hoped to be able to come out and arrange some assistance for you, but your men rode on too quickly."

"I am only a lieutenant, sir, but your courtesy in assuming a higher rank is flattering. What assistance did you have in mind?"

Mr. Goddard almost gasped at the directness of the question. "Well, it's too late, so we don't need…Oh, some forage for your mounts, some food for your men…"

"How much did you have in mind in each of those categories, sir? We will be most grateful. Of course, our commissary will reimburse any citizen for goods supplied in bulk."

Goddard's eyes bulged and his mouth went dry. He fumbled for his cigars to gain a moment to think. "Cigar, Lieutenant? Matches, matches," he mumbled, struggling for time.

The lieutenant's hand dropped to the flap of the big brown holster at his belt, and Goddard stepped back quickly, his face pale.

The lieutenant's face did not change a flicker, nor did he speak. He merely pulled a packet of matches out with his left hand and reached across to strike one on the butt of the big army colt that hung there. He offered the flaming match to Goddard in silence.

Gratefully, Goddard dropped his eyes to the flame and puffed importantly. "But it's too late now, is it not?" he said, his voice at a more relaxed, lower pitch.

"Oh, no, sir! I will inform the commissary, and he will come later to pick it all up. How much in each class of supply, sir?"

"Beg your pardon, sir, but a buggy is coming from the east," the mounted trooper interrupted.

Goddard's lungs filled with fresh, sweet morning air, and he took a full step backward with a sense of relief and barely suppressed anger at being bested by this Texan upstart in front of other citizens in the main street of his own town.

The lieutenant did not seem to notice Goddard's relief or rising anger. He seemed to no longer notice him at all. His fierce eyes focused on the approaching vehicle alone, his back turned to Mr. Goddard.

The fine roan mare held her head high and placed each hoof so precisely that she seemed to be dancing as the buggy whirled down the road from the east toward town. It was easy to see that the driver, a young female, was no stranger to handling a fine equipage at high speed with confidence. The approach was smooth, rapid, and beautiful to watch. The pace was checked firmly as the first houses were reached, and the light rig glided effortlessly to a stop before the lieutenant and Mr. Goddard. For a moment, there was silence to replace the sound of hooves and the rattle of wheels. A fine cloud of road dust washed up to the two men and broke like a wave, swirling forward to their feet.

The officer removed his hat and made a courteous bow while Mr. Goddard gave a less deep courtesy to this lady. She was surely a lady, and the prettiest Goddard believed he had ever seen. Brilliant blue eyes were wide set in a fair oval face with full lips and a short, straight nose. The curls that peeked from under her stylish bonnet were a honey blond. The figure was slender and straight but rounded and feminine. She was composed and aware of her high status, demure but not retiring. Her dress was a sky blue that complimented her coloring. Her voice, when she acknowledged their bows, was cultured, modulated, and musical.

"Miss Mary Ready, I presume?" the lieutenant asked. "We have been waiting for you. Here, boy, take charge of that animal!" he said to the servant riding on the back of the buggy facing to the rear. The man slipped to the ground and ran to take the mare's head and calm her restlessness.

"You have the advantage of me, sir. Who are you?"

"I am Lieutenant John McKenzie, sent to escort you safely to meet your uncle. May I also present Mr. Goddard of this town, who is a friend to our cause." This last remark was barely acknowledged by Miss Ready, but it caused a murmur among Ed and his friends and one or two other townspeople who were still enjoying the excitement of this unusual activity in their sleepy hamlet.

"But, where is my escort, sir? Surely you and one other of your men are not all there is. My uncle, General Morgan, promised me faithfully that his finest men should escort me into Louisville. Is he in such straits that he has only two fine men in his army?"

This last remark elicited a start from John McKenzie even bigger than the electric response that it got from Mr. Goddard and the townspeople within hearing.

"It was necessary that they ride on ahead in order for us to accomplish our other task."

"And what other task could be so important that it takes precedence over a solemn promise made by a gentleman to a lady, sir?" There was a razor edge on the word "sir."

"The protection of the army is the first charge of its cavalry, miss," he said stiffly.

"Ah," she said.

Mr. Goddard was bemused. "How the mighty have fallen!" he mused. "This slip of a girl has him in full retreat even quicker than he routed me. This could be valuable to me as well as fun to watch." He stepped a little closer to be sure that he missed not a word. Glancing around, he noticed that Ed and his friends, as well as the townspeople, were also edging closer. The mounted trooper was half smiling, half wincing as he listened.

McKenzie's face was scarlet. His eyes flashed. His jaw muscles twitched like snakes as he choked off a response that came out as a muted growl. He lowered his head and clapped his hat hard onto it. When he raised his face to speak again, she was smiling an angelic, innocent smile at him, her eyebrows raised inquiringly. He bowed his head and took a breath. When he raised his face to her again, he spoke quickly in a soft voice, the effort at control plainly evident in it.

Behind him, the trooper pulled his hat low over his eyes and covered a broad grin with his other hand and a glance to the side. One of Ed's friends snickered audibly. All of the bystanders' faces wore broad grins.

"Miss Ready, I implore you, we must move on to catch up with the escort."

"Had you not been so rude, we would not be compelled to hurry so. But, we must all show Christian charity and endure with a good heart what we cannot change. Scipio, check the harness and get in the back. We shall be ready as soon as that is accomplished, Mr. McKenzie."

Her answer from McKenzie sounded very like "harrrhuum-mmm!" but she smiled angelically nevertheless.

"What a woman," thought Mr. Goddard, as the lieutenant turned and mounted his charger.

"George, I want you on point two hundred yards in advance. Miss Ready, if you will keep pace with me, I would be obliged."

When she nodded her assent, he spurred his charger to a rack and followed the galloping trooper west across the bridge and north on the road to Louisville.

Mr. Goddard watched the tiny cavalcade out of sight along the road north. Without taking his eyes from the place where they were lost from view, he told Ed, "Catch my horse and get him saddled as fast as you can! I need to be on the road in ten minutes."

"Where you goin' in such a hurry, Mr. Goddard? I bet you ain't even had your breakfast yet, have you? That was really something, wasn't it? That little girl had him buffaloed faster than he had you..." Ed realized that he had gone too far when Mr. Goddard turned on him with a malevolent look that would have peeled the paint off of a porch swing. "I'll have him saddled in just a minute for you, Mr. Goddard. You'll see how quick I can be."

"Well, get about it then, now!" the banker snapped, as he jammed his cigar into his mouth and strode off for his house.

Ed looked back to see if Goddard was still watching his progress, and hurried on his task. The last baleful look had frightened him. He knew Goddard to be mean as he could be and no friend to any man. He also remembered that Goddard held a mortgage on his land and house, which Ed had little prospect of paying off. One thing did confuse him about the morning, though. It was that comment the officer made about "bein' a friend to our cause." He knew Goddard well enough to know that if he was going to sell anything to anybody, he was going to make a good profit on it. Forage and food. Where was he goin' to get that? When he got through with that damned mean horse of Goddard's, he'd go talk to Pete and Charley and some of the other folks about it and see if they could figure it out. That damned horse was almost as mean as Goddard was.

Goddard slammed the door when he entered his house and trotted upstairs. He paused a moment to collect his thoughts as he reached into his pocket for the key to unlock the door to Elizabeth's room.

"Are you all right, my dear? The danger is over. It was just a small party of cavalry passing through. They meant us no harm. I was able to hurry them along to reduce the danger to our town."

"Yes, dear. I was watching from the window. They seemed like such nice boys even with all of the guns and knives and things. Their officer was such a handsome young man. Was he well spoken, dear? He seemed a complete gentleman. And the girl in the buggy! What a young and pretty thing she was. Did you ever see such skin? It was like peaches and cream. I wish they could have stopped for a visit."

"No, dear, they had to go on to Louisville." She did not miss a thing, did she? He noted to himself. "We could not do such a thing as invite them in. It would be very bad. I understand that Anson

Grimes, the United States provost marshal with the army at Lexington, has arrested many citizens of standing as Rebel sympathizers for just such behavior."

Elizabeth still looked disappointed. From her window, four houses away from the intersection, she had recognized those youngsters as persons of social standing equal to her own—but not his. It made him more determined to bring them down. He would ride and not spare the whip to the telegraph station on the L & N Railroad just six miles west over the ridge and get a message to the army at Lexington. When they found out that the whole Rebel army was moving on to Louisville rather than to Lexington, where everyone thought it was going to attack, they would be very grateful. They might even brevet him a colonel or something like that. "Colonel Goddard." He liked it. It had a nice ring to it and would be valuable after the war, too.

"I have to run over to the telegraph office, Elizabeth, but I should be back by dinner time."

"But, dear, you haven't even had your breakfast yet. You will be hungry. I worry about you so when you don't take care of yourself. I will have Mandy make you something."

"No, no, I haven't got time. I have to send a message…" he paused and thought quickly. She must not know what message he was sending. She would be hurt and angry. It was not politics to Elizabeth; it all came down to those two young people in the street. She liked them on sight. Those she liked were the objects of constant, gentle, loving attention. It was what made him love her so. She could not know that he had done anything that might ultimately hurt them. It would hurt her, and her hurt was the only pain that he could not bear. "I have to order some things that I did not expect to need quite so soon. So I must get it off immediately. You do understand, don't you?"

She nodded her understanding and held her cheek up to be kissed. As he walked out of the room, he saw that she had turned back to the window. She was looking at the empty intersection as though it were still peopled with the little pageant of such a few minutes ago.

Chapter 2

The United States Army encampment at Lexington was an anthill of activity. Thousands of troops drilled in the open fields; wagons lined the roads into the city, bringing provisions and equipment to sustain the powerful force. Lines of white tents in pastures made an ivory necklace around the city. At houses commandeered for military headquarters, smartly uniformed sentinels walked their posts under the brilliant flowers of national and regimental flags.

The provost marshal, Colonel Anson Grimes, had his office in the city jail. It was close to the city hall where the army headquarters was located, and it allowed him to keep a close eye on the Rebel sympathizers whom he had locked up there. He just did not trust the local sheriff to pen up his neighbors so that the flow of information out of Lexington to the rebels could be shut off. He had done this in every town that the army had occupied, and it had proven to be very profitable for the army and for him. He had been able to find out about property where debt was heavy and buy it right out from under the "Secesh" while they were in no position to fight back. He promptly resold the property at a nice profit but still below its real value. When this war was over, he was going home a rich man.

Brigadier General Martin Hurlburt, the Intelligence chief, would not approve, but Anson Grimes didn't care a bit. He just kept his mouth shut about it and gave Hurlburt enough "spies" to keep him happy. He had been a policeman in a big eastern city force, and he did not think much of the Pinkertons who were collecting information for the Army. He brushed the cigar ashes off of the front of his uniform and stuffed his new list of spies and sympathizers into his pocket. He had to get the list approved by Hurlburt before he could make the arrests. "The sooner the better," he thought. "We won't be here forever, and there are a few more pieces of property that I want to pick up and resell before we leave."

He heaved himself out of his chair, found his hat, and lumbered out the door. The walk was a short one, but the sun hurt his eyes, and the stair to the third floor made him puff as he heaved his bulk upward. When he entered the spymaster's office, Captain Michaelman, the general's aide-de-camp, looked up unenthusiastically. The young man rose but did not speak. "The general in?" He almost added "Sonny," but he decided to not further antagonize someone who was already nearly an inveterate enemy. Might make him inquisitive. He was a smart lawyer. Anson always thought it was better to stay away from lawyers unless you could buy them.

"I'll let him know that you are here," was all Michaelman said as he rose, opened the general's office door, and went in, closing it behind himself.

"That fat crook, Grimes, is outside. I am sure that he has his list of Rebel sympathizers with him again. I think there is something funny going on here, General."

"If the 'funny' is civil law, we have no jurisdiction."

"When martial law is declared, we will have." Captain Michaelman smiled as he said it.

"What do you know, Jimmy, that I ought to know? Something is going on, isn't there?"

"I am quartered with Arthur Smith from the general staff. He told me that martial law would be declared if there were a major Rebel attack on Louisville. The purpose is to give us legal authority to lock up all of the suspected Rebels to maintain control of the city during an attack. The decree will apply to all of Kentucky, not to the city alone. Then we could catch Grimes red-handed, try him, and hang him all in a matter of days."

"Why do we, in general, and you in particular, have any interest in this thing?"

"Several reasons. There are two lists coming in to us of Rebel sympathizers. One from him and one from the Pinkertons. Some people are on both lists. I concede that those are probably Rebel sympathizers. Of those on Grimes's list, several always lose valuable property. That never happens to those who appear only on the list from the Pinkertons. We are interested in catching real spies and supporters of the rebellion. We are not interested in antagonizing honest citizens of the state to make enemies out of them."

"How do you know about the property?"

"A Princeton classmate of mine is in jail on Grimes's orders. He told me what was common knowledge among the prisoners there. I went down to the deed records here in the courthouse to check it out. Some of the sale documents are clearly forged." Captain Michaelman raised his hand to stop the general's forming question. "Many of the signatures are in the same hand—the hand that writes out Grimes's list. If we can get him to acknowledge that he prepares the list personally, and if we can find one of these transactions, after martial law is declared, we have caught him red-handed."

General Hurlburt sank low in his chair and stared thoughtfully at the fresh cigar in his hand. He did not like Anson Grimes, nor did he trust him all that much. He knew young Michaelman to be spotlessly honest, but he wondered if there were more going on here that he might not be aware of. The mention of the Princeton classmate bothered him. He could not figure it out completely.

"Are you saying that we should not be confiscating the property of these damned Rebels?"

Michaelman looked bemused. "Not at all, sir. I think it should be confiscated and sold to pay us back for the war. What I object to is personal enrichment of individuals because of their positions. I object to forgery. I object to false swearing, and I object to the abuse of good citizens by officials to make a personal profit. You are worried about my mention of my friend in jail as a sympathizer, are you not?"

"Let me explain. Harry Montgomery visited me in New York just before the war broke out. He was there to buy rifles for the South. He told me all of this, but assured me of his lasting friendship. We agreed that if we met on the battlefield, we would try the issue with the sword, and we agreed that we would each do all in our power to defeat the other's cause. The battles over and victory reached, whatever the issue, we would resume our friendship as before. It is the only way that he wanted it and the only way that I would agree to it. He is in jail now and will stay there. He is a man of formidable ability. We cannot have him working against us. I will do what I can do to soften the severity of his confinement but not to end it."

"Fair enough!" the general grunted. "Show Anson Grimes in, and we will see what can be done to clean our own stable."

Grimes felt restless and sullen. He wondered what had taken so long. These two might be cooking up something. He'd watch his step.

As he entered the general's office, there was a loud clatter of boots and spurs on the stair. Both Michaelman and Grimes rushed to the head of the stair to see what was going on. Looking down the stairwell, they saw Sergeant Hall, their dispatch rider, taking the stairs two at a time. His boots were banging on each step in counterpoint to the clash of his sword and scabbard on the stone steps as he rushed upward. He reached the third floor landing almost as soon as they reached the head of the stairs.

"What is it? What have you got?" Michaelman demanded.

"For the general, sir. Three messages that he will be mighty glad to have!"

Michaelman simply turned on his heel and gestured to the others to follow. As they entered General Hurlburt's office, Sergeant Hall stepped in front of his desk and remembered to salute. He pulled three sheets of paper from the leather pouch at his waist and handed them to the general.

Martin Hurlburt took the sheets and scanned them quickly. Then he read them slowly again. A third time he read them after sorting them into a new sequence. Silently he got up and walked to the map of Kentucky on his wall. Consulting the messages again, he scanned the map intently until he had tapped it in three places. "These times on each message, what do they represent?"

"Those marked at the top are the times of receipt at our Signal

Corps office at the train depot, General. The time at the end of the text is the receipt time of the transmission by the L & N operator sending to Lexington. We cannot tell exactly when the events described in the three messages occurred, other than by a reasonable guess at the time it would take to travel from one town to the next. The last message includes the phrase "a few minutes ago." The town from which it was sent is only two miles away from the railroad, so the difference between the receipt time by the L & N operator and the actual event is probably no more than a half hour or so."

Michaelman and Grimes looked back and forth at the general and the sergeant, waiting for some information as to what was going on. Hurlburt passed the three sheets to Grimes, who read them and passed each on to Captain Michaelman. His face clouded then cleared. When he looked up, he seemed relaxed and back in control. Hurlburt looked at him, inquisitively asking a question without speaking.

Grimes tossed his head and spoke. "I don't believe it, but I think we ought to act on it. This says the Rebels are headed for Louisville. We know they are coming here. They want the manpower around here, the horses, the forage, the crops, and the road net. We have been sure of that for a long time. Besides, Louisville is too big a bite for the whole Rebel army of the Tennessee, let alone that horse thief John Hunt Morgan."

"Jimmy, what do you think?" the general asked.

"I think it probably is true. It is too much luck, but sometimes that does happen in wars. If we had time, we could trace back to the originator of one of these messages. The other two are not traceable to any single person beyond the telegrapher, but they are eyewitness reports that can be readily checked in the event something is ... shall we say 'wrong with them.' I don't think people would set themselves up to be caught so easily."

"Grimes, you say that you don't believe them, but we ought to move anyway? That does not make sense. That would put this whole army in motion away from the point that we believe to be his real target."

"If the messages are real, we must move right now to allow

enough time for the march from here to Louisville. Morgan may be even closer to Louisville than we are. Our army is big enough to defeat him if he attacks us. Also, there are already fortifications in plenty all around Louisville. If we don't move and the Rebels take Louisville unopposed, the best thing that will happen to us will be to be sent home in disgrace as a bunch of fools. I don't have to describe the worst thing that may happen. You can probably already feel a tightness in your throat."

Grimes rubbed his face with his stubby fingers. "If we stay, he would be a fool to attack us. He will march all over this part of Kentucky recruiting regiments while we cower behind our breast works waiting for him to do just what we want. He won't do that, not John Morgan. He will taunt us until we start to come out and then attack the lead elements stretched out on the road, beat hell out of the lead division, and ride away victorious. If you try to march out deployed in line of battle, he will stay out of range until you get exhausted and then hit you hard when you are all worn out, beat hell out of a brigade or so, and ride off the victor. We have more than fifty correspondents here from papers all over our country and Europe. What do you suppose your skin will be worth then, just because you ignored a false lead? The point is that we don't run this army, but as the intelligence and spy catchers, we'll get blamed whatever goes wrong."

"I can't fault your opinion of what Morgan is likely to do, but I hear you telling me that we should get the general to move to save our own necks?"

Anson Grimes smiled grimly. "Our own necks are literally what I want to save."

Captain Michaelman turned away from the window where he had been listening. "I agree with Colonel Grimes, but I think that he did not go far enough. We can alert our cavalry for a forced march back to Lexington if Morgan comes this way. They can engage him and hold him until the rest of the army comes up. Second, we need to send out a small force of cavalry to go to the places these messages came from. A troop of well-mounted cavalry can travel fast enough to investigate the one man who is identifiable in these messages. If he is found to be a Rebel sympathizer, we can telegraph the news to wherever the Army is, bring the man in, hang him as an object lesson, and confiscate all of his property. I think Colonel Grimes is the perfect man to do that job. Under martial law, which we can get the general commanding to declare as soon as we march, all of the authority that we need to deal with our problems will be available to us. Colonel Grimes, I should also ask if you have any more to report to us today. We have to move quickly."

Anson Grimes smiled as he handed over his new list. He was seeing all sorts of possibilities in the situation. "Here it is. Wrote it up this morning myself."

General Hurlburt's head snapped up. "Yes, yes. Good for you, Colonel. I need to see the commanding general right away. You two get things moving while I am gone." He scooped up the three messages and walked briskly out the door and down the stairs to the first floor offices of the commanding general.

"Well, Colonel, we need to get moving. I will get orders issued for a company of cavalry to be placed under your orders for your expedition to check out these messages. It makes sense to start with the closest town first and work back to the farthest, since the only person identified is in the farthest town. That way you should know for sure what really happened and can match it to the reports. I will have copies made of the three messages and send them over to you as soon as General Hurlburt returns. I will also get a copy of the martial law proclamation for you to have with you. I plan to send Sergeant Hall with you to represent us. You will probably want to take some of your men, too. Please don't reduce the guard too much. I want enough force to hold the prisoners if need be. Is there anything else you need?"

Anson Grimes was about to tell this smart rich kid what he thought but decided against it. Michaelman had given him everything he wanted. Sergeant Hall was no threat. He seemed to be just a token representative. "No, that seems to be all that I need. I will leave Lieutenant Higgins with you to take care of the day-to-day business of the jail. He does that for me, so there should be no surprises or escapes for you to have to cope with." Without waiting for any acknowledgment from the captain, he walked out.

Chapter 3

The army began its march with the departure of a large cavalry force a few hours later. Tents were struck. Equipment was packed and loaded into wagons harnessed to braying, protesting mules. Blue clad infantry marched out of trampled, empty fields, followed by white-topped supply wagons. Gun parks emptied their glistening brass cannon, limbers, and gun carriages on to the road, adding the thunder of their wheels and clink of harness to the martial symphony of tramping feet and shouted commands.

It was four o'clock in the morning before the last units cleared the boundaries of the old camp. One infantry regiment with a battery of artillery and a troop of cavalry was all that was left in and around Lexington of the mighty army that had gripped it so tightly and flooded its streets with Yankee soldiers.

After breakfast that morning, an immature-looking young man named Achilles Quintas Wallace shed the uniform of a Confederate private and put on the slightly-too-small clothes of a young teenage boy. He walked out of the house where he had been hiding for a week and loitered down the street toward the depot. With numerous stops to throw rocks at puddles, squirrels, and various other opportune targets, he arrived at the telegraph office. He handed the crumpled paper and some coins to the operator and remarked that his Mama had told him to wait for an answer.

The operator agreed to send the message in a few minutes and call him when the reply came in. 'Chilles Wallace nodded his head and went outside. He pulled out a clasp knife, picked up a stick, and began to whittle while he listened to the Morse code messages

coming and going over the wire. Although he interrupted his whit-
tling once to throw a rock at a cat stalking a bird, he clearly heard
all of the military messages coming and going, as well as his own
message, which read, "Fever broke last night, but Grandmother
wants to see you. Can you come?" and the answer, which said, "I
will come as fast as I can. Leaving later today."

When he was summoned about a half hour later and given the
text of the reply, 'Chilles thanked the telegrapher for his help and
walked back toward the jail. He needed to see what was still there
after all of the troops left. Later he would go out the road to the
southwest to the stream and fish a bit while he watched the size
and dispositions of the Federal picket stationed there.

By mid afternoon of the next day, Anson Grimes and his force had
been through the northern-most towns that had sent messages to
his army. He found out more details about the reports that were
interesting. Some were helpful. Others were only curious. First, the
Rebel cavalry detachment of about thirty men had indeed passed
through. They had stopped in one town to water horses and in the
other to get a nail reset in the hoof of the horse that pulled the
buggy. The woman in the buggy was young and pretty. She was
very talkative and repeatedly mentioned Louisville. The officer in
charge of the cavalry troop had done his level best to make her
be silent, but in the last town, he had provoked a volcanic burst
of temper that still had the locals laughing. The local wags would
say in a female voice, "You, *sir*...are no gentleman!" and would
hold their sides and break into gales of laughter. The target of this
abuse, the Rebel officer, seemed to have been completely at a loss
as to how to make her stop giving valuable military information to
everybody and sundry. The whole thing seemed to be a great stroke
of luck for the Union. He had another ten miles to ride to get to
Cranmer, but he wanted to get there today so that he could check
the final link in the chain. He sent a telegraph back to Captain
Michaelman describing what he had found so far as well as his
plan for tomorrow.

Later that evening, over to the north and west of the three
towns in a sparsely settled area, a division of Confederate cavalry

was preparing to move. The last tent left standing as they broke camp was General John Hunt Morgan's tent. Morgan was not alone. In addition to his usual staff, there was present an older gentleman in civilian clothes. His empty left sleeve and the terrible angry scars on his face testified to the toll of recent battles.

Major Homer Montgomery had been in the Second Kentucky Infantry of the Confederate Army under Colonel Roger Hanson at Fort Henry and Fort Donelson in February. He led the infantry attack on the Federal battery in the failed attempt to break out of the encircling Federal forces. He had fallen at the mouth of the guns as his men, supported by Bedford Forrest, had swarmed over the red-hot barrels. The lithe black man, Caesar, who now stood behind his chair had helped him off the field on Forrest's horse. The general and the major talked as old friends about the events of the last few months and about the possibilities of the future. A staff officer interrupted them, entering the tent and reporting that the patrol had returned. In a few minutes, the sound of hooves and the clatter of wheels announced the arrival of a party outside of the tent. Morgan rose and extended a hand to his old friend to assist him to his feet.

The staff officer pulled back the tent flap and announced, "Miss Cynthia Montgomery and Lieutenant John McKenzie!"

Her blue dress was a bit dusty, but the marks of travel had not dimmed her brilliant eyes and smile. She was as bright and vivacious as ever, and she seemed to be sharing some private joke with Lieutenant McKenzie.

The sight of her made General Morgan beam and made her father's face light from within as though the physical pain of his wounds had left him magically. The general bowed to her gracefully and kissed her hand, for John Hunt Morgan was ever the gentleman. Homer Montgomery clasped his beautiful daughter to himself and pressed her close. Lieutenant McKenzie saluted and reported to Morgan. The general motioned to all to be seated, and asked, "Well, John, how did it go?"

A few minutes of earnest explanation described in detail the deception that they had practiced on the townspeople along their route. He also apologized for inventing a niece for the general's wife, explaining that he believed it would give more of a rationale for Miss Montgomery's knowledge of military plans. Morgan laughed, and remarked that he was sure that Mattie Ready Morgan loved a joke better than anyone else.

"Did you catch anyone out, John?"

"One Albert Goddard of Cranmer is now badly compromised with his friends as a friend to our cause. If the Yankees don't get him first, we can deal with him when we are next in town. No citizen of the other towns was careless enough to put himself in such a situation. The people of the towns were kindness itself. At each halt, there were pitchers of milk, and small things to eat were generously offered to the troopers. Knowing our people, I expect the same is offered to the Yankee soldiers, too."

Morgan nodded and replied, "Yes, I am sure they do. You will be pleased to hear that your stratagem was successful. The Yankees are on the march for Louisville. The town is practically unguarded. We are leaving now. I want you to rest your men and horses and then catch up with us by noon tomorrow. We expect to hit them just after dark. Colonel Gano has more work for his Texas Rangers." Morgan belted on his pistol and saber, kissed Cynthia Montgomery's hand once more, and shook the major's hand. Then, patting John McKenzie on the shoulder in acknowledgment of his salute, he strode out of the tent and mounted his charger. His instructions to leave the tent up as long as the major needed it were clearly overheard.

There was a moment of stillness in the tent and then bubbling laughter from all. When the merriment ebbed, Major Montgomery asked, "Have you heard from my dear cousin, John?"

"Yes, Uncle Homer, I got a letter three weeks ago from Mother. She is well. She is saddened by the suffering and separation brought on by the war, but firm to maintain the right. She particularly asked that I pass her love to you when I saw you. She was very distressed to hear of your wounds. She said she was proud to hear of your rescue by Caesar, but she was not surprised. She did ask after you and Scipio especially, Caesar."

"Thank you, Marse John! Your Mama is a fine lady, always kind and generous to me. You tell her that I'll always take good care of the major."

"Now Uncle Homer, I have some unpleasant news for you."

"Good Lord, John, what can that be?"

"I must reveal that this war has made your lovely daughter into a scold and no lady."

"Why, John McKenzie! I'll show you a scold!" Her fair cheeks flushed pink, but the laughter from her father and her cousin quenched the fire immediately. When it was done, she said that they must be gone on their way, as they had a long road before they were in safe territory.

When all were safely in the buggy and Caesar and Scipio were well mounted and armed as outriders, John tapped Caesar on the leg and motioned him to bend low. "Be careful as you go, Caesar. One of you stay well in front of the rig. We have no patrols on the roads to the south and west, so anyone that you meet in the dark is not friendly. Do you have a weapon for Scipio? I never saw one on the trip."

"Yes, Marse John. The major got his navy colt, I got a carbine and two holster pistols, and Scipio has a double barrel shotgun. He had it hidden under the sackin' he was sittin' on. I sho' would like a pair of navy or army colts for me and Scipio 'stead of these single shot pistols if you can get them fo' me."

John laughed. "I'll get you both a pair in Lexington day after tomorrow, Caesar."

After last sad goodbyes, the little convoy rode off into the darkness.

Chapter 4

The blue cavalry rode tentatively into Cranmer with Colonel Anson Grimes well to the rear of the column. Ed did not see them until they were across the bridge because they came from the opposite direction. He did notice the difference in the way they came into town. Instead of a couple of riders who came in and looked everybody over, the whole troop rode in a close column. The troopers seemed tense, and while they looked at everybody who was on the street, there were no smiles or greetings. It was easy for Ed to decide to stay on his front step peeling potatoes for supper.

Before the cavalry dismounted, the captain sent several troopers out each of the three roads just as the gray cavalry had done. There were four who came to dismount in front of Ed's house at the edge of town, and a fifth came along a minute or so later. Ed watched them get settled, and when one walked up and asked for some firewood to cook their supper on, he gave them several logs. The fifth man, a sergeant, came over and sat down by Ed. He introduced himself as Gerry Hall, offered Ed some tobacco from his pouch, and packed his own pipe as he and Ed chatted companionably about the weather and farming. Ed asked if he was a farmer before the war. Hall answered that he grew up on a farm in Ohio, but was teaching school when the war started. Gerry Hall asked no questions and chatted pleasantly for a half an hour or so before Ed felt bold enough to ask him what had brought the Union Cavalry here. He immediately regretted the question and apologized, but Hall was not the least bit put off by the question.

"We are here looking for friends," he answered candidly.

27

"Everybody hereabouts is friendly," responded Ed innocently.

"Yes, they seem to be. Most folks are, but I meant friends to the Union."

Ed looked blank.

"Secession is a terrible evil and it must be defeated. We are looking for those who are true friends to the Union. I mean friends who have a stake in victory. Is there anybody like that here?"

This was dangerous ground for Ed. His mind raced, and he wished that he had finished peeling the spuds and gone inside before this fellow got here. He said lamely, "Some of our boys went off to join the army."

"Of course, and that's very fine, but I really meant something different. People like you and me don't have much to give. I was young and joined up. You are a lot older and needed to keep farming to keep the country supplied with food." (Ed visibly relaxed.) "But, there are some prominent people who don't seem to have made up their minds yet. For instance, I noticed a bank here in town. Now, that's something that will really help a community. Who is the banker?"

"That's Mr. Goddard. He lives just down the street about six houses."

"Is he like most bankers?" asked Sergeant Hall.

Ed laughed. "Yep, I guess so."

"Ever heard him say anything about helping one side or the other?"

"Well, I always thought he was a Union man, because he was always talkin' about the war bein' bad for business and such like."

"That doesn't mean very much. Everybody says that. I guess you got to watch what they do more than what they say. The Rebs have been all over this part of Kentucky. What did he act like when they were here?"

"Generally, he stays inside his house 'til they leave, just like he's doing now."

"I'll bet he never comes out."

"He did once, and I can tell you I was sure surprised. He wanted me to go ask a bunch of questions of a Confederate cavalry officer a few days ago, but then he came out of his house and talked to the man himself. I was mighty glad 'cause I didn't want to talk to any officer askin' him questions, I don't care which side he's on."

"You and me both, Brother! I try to stay away from them myself."

"Goddard must be a pretty brave man. What did he talk to this Reb about?" Hall asked casually.

Ed got a bit wary again, so he answered, "I didn't hear exactly what he said. The officer just said something like he was friendly. No, that wasn't it. It was something like 'he's friends with our cause.' Everybody noticed 'cause nobody around here describes Mr. Goddard as friendly. I mean he's nice enough, but he ain't easy," Ed ended lamely, and he wished he had not said anything. "You ain't going to do anythin' to him are you?"

Sergeant Hall shook his head. "Who? Me? No. I just do my job and let the officers worry about stuff like that. This Goddard must be a typical banker. Everybody owes him money, and everybody is a little scared of him. Some bankers are real good folks. Some are mean as hell. He sounds a bit like he's in the second bunch.

"Well, I got to go visit the other outposts. Thanks for the wood for the cook fires." Hall dusted off the seat of his britches as he rose to go. "Maybe I'll see you in the morning."

Ed felt relieved when the soldier left. He seemed friendly enough, but he was different. He didn't talk or act as if he had been farm people. Ed shrugged and went inside. He dropped the latch in place for the first time in months and lay down on his bed in his clothes.

When it was full dark and Sergeant Hall had visited each outpost to see if there were any civilians present, he walked quietly back to the house that Colonel Anson Grimes had commandeered as his resting place. He found Grimes sitting in a comfortable chair in the parlor of the house. He had some papers spread out on a small table before him.

"What did you find out?" His deep voice sounded tired and irritated.

"I talked to three people. A man named Ed Barton knew the most. None of the three would admit to hearing Goddard say anything that would be useful to us, but they all agreed that

Goddard had some private words with a Rebel officer. They also agree that the Reb introduced him to the girl as a friend to our cause. All were very careful to not stand out against Goddard. All probably owe him money. I thought that they might be saying such things about him out of spite, but the observations of each were too close together to be other than true."

Anson Grimes smiled. It was not a happy or friendly smile.

"Write that up in a report. I told the captain of this troop that I want to be out of here before first light in the morning. Goddard is going with us under arrest. I'll finish with him when we get to Lexington. When the troop stands-to at four in the morning, go arrest him. Get his own horse saddled for him to ride and bring him here to me."

Sergeant Hall acknowledged the order with a salute and left to locate Goddard's house and stable.

By noon the next day, the troop with its prisoner was well on the way back toward Lexington. A miserable Albert Goddard rode slumped in the middle of the troop with a trooper on either side of him and Sergeant Hall behind him. After two hours of complaining that he had always been a good Union man, he gave up and fell silent. He mentally listed anyone he knew who might be in the state government. The list was small, but it might help. He was in agony of spirit over poor Elizabeth's cries as he was taken away. Old Mrs. Tyler from across the street had slapped her way through the arresting detail of soldiers to take her in her arms and comfort her. He could not figure out why they had arrested him, unless it was that conversation with the Confederate cavalry officer and the pretty girl that they were using against him.

The cavalry patrol with Grimes and his prisoner finally reached the outskirts of Lexington about an hour after dark. They were challenged and passed by the picket where the road crossed the small stream. The troop came through at a walk, and the picket soldiers turned back to their campfires and supper. There was a short break in the column, and another body of about thirty men followed the patrol through the guard, silently slouched in their saddles after a long day's ride.

About a half hour later, a body of infantry marched into the picket's position from the town side of the bridge. When they were challenged by the soldier on that part of the road, an irritated voice replied, "When are these men going to learn how to properly give a challenge and response! Sergeant, get that man's name!" The befuddled soldier stammered, "Sorry, sir."

The sergeant advancing toward him asked that he step out of the way, and then shoved a big pistol under his chin and ordered him to be silent or die. By then, a warning would have done no good. The "infantry" broke ranks and rushed silently into the picket and captured every man without firing a shot. There was a low whistle from the Confederate officer in charge of the assault party, and within moments, a long column of cavalry trotted through the captured outpost toward town.

The column broke into segments as it came to the edge of town. At each street, a portion of the men followed an officer to some destination. The few Union soldiers who were out walking the streets at this late hour paid little attention to the cavalry patrols coming in from their work. At the city hall and at the jail, the sentinels straightened up at the approach of troops under command of an officer, but they did little else until the officers commanding each party gave the command to halt and dismount. By then it was too late to do much. The officer and sergeant passed the reins of their horses to a private and briskly marched up to the sentinels. When the sentinel challenged them, pistols came out and were pressed against bellies so quickly that they hardly had time to react. At the jail, one provost guard had time to pull the trigger of his musket and let off a shot that hit no one. The dismounted troops in the street rushed the door. On the lower floors, the occupants were overwhelmed quickly, but the shot, the shouting, and noise of the rush gave notice to the Union officers and soldiers higher up the stairs, and shots started coming down the stairs from above. The Confederates were better organized, and a volley from a squad of cavalrymen suppressed the fire from above long enough for the raiders to rush the stairway and gain command of the halls on each floor. Then there were demands for surrender as the gray soldiers went from room to room overpowering the isolated defenders.

Colonel Anson Grimes was warned by the commotion of the invasion of his jail. He ran to the door and locked it. Then he went to his desk and got the two ledgers that he used to record his property dealings and put them outside his window on the ledge. He used his weight and strength to push his desk in front of the door to his office and doused the lights. He went to the window and looked out, but a shot from the street made him pull back from the opening quickly. First, he thought to hide inside the roll top desk but rejected the idea when he heard shooting that he knew must be through doors. The thought of a big minie ball smashing through the door and desk into his body appalled him. He decided to crouch in the corner of the room closest to the door and hope they would not search the room.

The building had quieted down considerably when an authoritative rap on the door startled him out of his rising hope that he would be ignored. There was a command to open the door and come out with his hands up. His silence was answered by the thunder of a shot that shattered the door lock. When a kick on the door showed that some object blocked it, he heard a gritty voice shout for him to unblock the door and come out immediately or they would come in shooting.

"No! Don't shoot! I'll come out." He pushed at the desk and slid his big Starr revolver out the door on the floor. He walked out very slowly with his hands well up in the air. The grim faces that surrounded him began to smile when they saw his colonel's eagles. The smiles became even broader when a Confederate entered his office and called out the news gathered from the papers on his desk that he was the provost marshal. He was promptly hustled down to the basement where the cells were being emptied of Confederates and filled with Union soldiers.

John McKenzie walked into Grimes's office and began to search through his papers. He put several files and ledgers into a gunnysack to be carried away. The rest of the papers that had no military value he threw into the fireplace and set them on fire. He turned and looked around the room for a safe or other secure place that might hold confidential information. There was none to be found. This was so unusual that he began to look around the office more closely. He went back to the desk and pulled out all of the drawers. He tapped and measured the top and sides to check for concealed compartments. He found nothing. He looked through the saddlebags thrown on the floor in the corner and found a sheaf of notes on one Albert Goddard. This brought a smile to John's face. He added the papers to his sack of valuable documents. Turning, he took one more look around the room. The window was open. There was a bullet hole from the outside in the glass. Why had the Yankee provost marshal been at the window? Good sense alone would have kept him away from it. John leaned out and looked down. There was a clear view of the street in both directions, and there on the ledge in the shadows were two ledgers. John scooped them up and added them to the sack and moved down to the basement.

As John entered the cell block, a familiar voice called his name. "John, it's me, Harry!"

John turned to see Harry Montgomery among the Confederates being let out of the cells. "Harry, I am so glad I found you. I need your help. Please stand by Sergeant O'Brien and tell him which people here are in jail for being Confederates and which are here because they are criminals."

"I'll be glad to, but I want a word in private before we finish up about some of these people."

It was only a few minutes before the sorting of sheep from goats was done. Harry took John aside and told him about one Albert Goddard who had been put in the cell as a Confederate sympathizer, all the while protesting loudly his firm ties to the Union. John threw back his head and laughed. "Don't worry about him, Harry. I am already aware of Mr. Goddard and his sympathies. There is more to the story that I will tell you after we are on the road out of here. Trust me, it is the right thing to do to treat Mr. Albert Goddard as a friend of ours for the time being." Harry looked puzzled, but accepted the idea.

John McKenzie then went to the cell packed with Union soldiers. In a loud voice, he told them that all who would give their parole to not fight against the Confederacy until properly exchanged would be released to go to their homes to await exchange.

In a harsher tone, he told them that any who would not give their parole would be sent south to a prison camp. He also cautioned them that any person taking up arms and fighting before he was properly exchanged was subject to instant execution upon recapture. He was gratified to find all of the blue soldiers quite ready to go home for a while and rest. He did give instruction to his clerk to be sure that the officers, in particular, were properly identified and that their signatures were legible.

The command stayed in Lexington for two days, and during that time they got enough volunteers to add five companies to the brigade. Richard Gano's squadron of Texas Cavalry became the Third Kentucky Cavalry with the addition of these men. When the outposts announced the approach of a large Union army toward Lexington, Morgan's cavalry mounted their fine Kentucky horses and slipped through the tightening net. Many of the former prisoners traveled with the command until they were out of the trap, and then they slipped off in their various directions to their homes or other safe places. John McKenzie gave Albert Goddard special attention until he was well clear of the approaching Union troops. He was even sped on his way with the advice to hurry on to his home to avoid recapture, as the Yankees would probably be very harsh if he were to be taken in again. This advice lent wings to his heels.

Chapter 5

Captain James Carthage Michaelman was appalled at the mess that he found in Lexington when the army returned. The stream of paroled Union soldier prisoners strolling gaily north toward their homes was bad enough. The loss of files and documents that had been left behind was even worse. A very nervous and agitated Anson Grimes met him at the jail and described to him the thorough looting of information files and the absolute destruction of some valuable records by the rebels. Grimes seemed to be very upset. He was more upset than Captain Michaelman had ever seen him. It made him wonder what else had happened to upset Grimes so much. He asked Grimes if he had escaped or been paroled by the Rebels, not satisfied that Grimes's answer was entirely clear. Grimes said something about barricading himself in his office and resisting, but there were no bullet holes in his door or anywhere else in his office except the shattered lock. He wondered what might be behind it, but other things occupied his mind at that moment. He looked at the list of prisoners who had been rescued from his jail, and he compared it with the list of his own men paroled. It was shocking what had happened in such a short time. He knew that the exchange of the paroled soldiers of his command would take place fairly soon. Nevertheless, it would be weeks before they could go home, report to a parolee camp, and be released to come back to work. In the meantime, he would have to carry all of the work himself. He walked back to his office and dropped into his chair with a long sigh.

One thing for which Michaelman was both happy and sorry

was the release of his friend Harry Montgomery. He wished that
Harry would stay home after his release, but he knew that Harry
would not do so. Harry was too good a friend for him to not wish
him in safety. On the other hand, Harry was too capable a man
for him to welcome the thought of having that agile mind and
undoubted ability working against the Union.

Those were all things that he could not control. He would have
to give up worrying about them and focus on the few things that
he could do by himself. He thought about the moves that he must
make to damage the ability of Morgan to move about the country
at will and to deceive the Union forces regarding his movements.
He had the names of two of Morgan's agents, and he was going
to have them hanged. He sat down and wrote out the draft for
two "wanted" handbills and entered names and descriptions as
well as a generous five hundred dollar reward. He decided to make
the reward payable in gold to increase the appeal to any hard-up
Rebel who might be tempted. He started to call for Sergeant Hall,
but realized that even Hall was on his way home on parole. He
shrugged and took the leaflets to the printer around the corner so
that they would be ready the next day.

Late the next morning, the printer's devil delivered the stacks
of handbills to his desk. He read the text critically.

WANTED!
The Man Known as
ALBERT GODDARD
Posing as a banker, this known Rebel agent
Is wanted by the United States Army for
Spying on the United States
And for
Giving Aid and Comfort to the
Enemy
$500 in GOLD
Will be paid to the person who
Turns him over to
Captain James Carthage Michaelman
At U.S. Army Headquarters in Lexington.

The second handbill was similar to the first.

WANTED!
The Woman Known as
MARY READY
About 21 years old, Blonde,
Of medium height and slender figure
Well spoken
The Name may not be her real name
She is a known **REBEL AGENT**
And is considered dangerous
She is a SPY and has actively
Aided the Rebel Army in the field
$500 in GOLD
Paid to the person who delivers her to
Captain James Carthage Michaelman
At U.S. Army Headquarters in Lexington.

Captain Michaelman gave the stack of handbills to his cavalry detachment with instructions to post them as far south as they could go around the countryside.

Albert Goddard made it home in almost record time. He had not ridden so hard in many years, but the fear of what was behind him and the anticipation of getting back to Elizabeth made him push his mount relentlessly. He had to remind himself to get rid of the horse before he got too close to home, since Lieutenant McKenzie had given him a cavalry horse with a clear U.S. brand on its rump. It seemed that he could not escape entanglement in the Rebels' cause no matter how loyal he was or how hard he tried. He decided to turn the horse loose before he came in sight of town and long before he crossed the river. He would walk into town from there. It would not cost him too much time and would be much safer.

Chapter 6

Cynthia Montgomery kept the buggy moving along at a nice trot. The horse was rested and well fed, and she had errands to run. She needed to get to the store to buy things for the house and kitchen, and she wanted to visit her friends in town. Caesar rode a saddle horse beside her, armed with a shotgun and pistol. He was her constant companion and protector whenever she left Palatine. The country was too unsettled for her to go about unescorted, her father maintained. The major's war council, Scipio and Caesar, agreed with him. She had come to accept the company and security that the presence of a formidable man like Caesar gave her. More than that, she had known him all of her life. His kindness and strength were a legend in the area, as was his loyalty to Major Montgomery. Although he had been born a slave, he had been freed for many years. He had been the major's right hand in the operation of the farms and property. The cooperation between Caesar, Scipio, and the major was smooth, seamless, and complete. They knew each other so well that communication of ideas and instructions was simple. Often, no instruction was necessary, as the responsible person acted on his own initiative. She could tell that Caesar was impatient with her and nervous about this trip. He had heard reports of Federal cavalry in the area that were arresting people for Southern sympathies on the flimsiest of evidence. Houses had been looted and burned, and blacks, both slave and free, had been herded off like cattle to work for the Union garrisons in the state. Nevertheless, it was late summer and things needed to be done. She had disregarded his earnest pleas to wait until the Yankee troops had moved on before making the journey. There were things they must have.

Her father and Scipio had been gone from the house with farm work when she made her decision. Caesar had dawdled and delayed in getting the buggy ready in hopes that they would return before Cynthia departed so that he could get more allies to support his caution, but they had not returned. Finally, he had no other choice but to arm himself and ride with her as escort. Throughout the trip, he pushed his horse to stay ahead of her to clear the way for her, but she constantly pressed in close behind him. His imperious signals for her to drop back did no good. She smiled a luminous smile and used her expert skill to keep the buggy close behind him, as if it were some sort of challenge or race.

They were not far from town where the road ran straight across a big meadow and then curved sharply to the right into a heavily wooded area. Caesar spurred his horse to a full gallop and waved her back again, but she applied the whip to her horse, expertly negotiated the bend in the road, and plunged into the shadow-darkened stretch of road through the forest. For a moment, she was blinded by the gloom after the bright sunlight of the meadow. Then she saw that the whole road was lined on both sides with blue uniformed soldiers. Horses were along and across the road blocking the way through.

Caesar pulled his mount up hard, and Cynthia stepped hard on the brake as she reined in. The horse sat on its haunches and struggled desperately to avoid running into the animals blocking its path. Dust clouds and clods of dirt flew forward and enveloped the buggy, Caesar, and the men in the road. After a long skid and a fierce struggle, the rig came to rest.

Two blue-coated troopers lay moaning in the ditch with the marks of the buggy wheels on their bodies or the terrible gashes delivered by flailing hooves. Horses plunged and kicked excitedly. Men scrambled to control their mounts and to avoid injury. Shouts, curses, and the thunder of stamping hooves filled the air.

It was several minutes before some calm began to return to the shadowy roadbed. A burly officer with captain's shoulder straps strode up and down the column rapping out instructions and orders to calm the confusion. He sent a sergeant to minister to the two injured men and, accompanied by a lieutenant and several privates, he approached the buggy and its shaken occupant. Caesar backed his quivering horse so that he was slightly in front of the buggy where he could get a clear view of the approaching officer.

"Well, miss. You have wounded two of my men and have done a great deal of damage. Why are you tearing about the country-side like the devil himself was after you? What are you running from? Or should I ask who are you running from?" His manner was neither kindly nor bantering when he asked his questions. His shoulders were hunched up and forward. His face was hard and pinched. The dark eyes under heavy brows glared at her, unblinking.

Cynthia Montgomery flushed scarlet, but she sat erect, controlling her consternation and anger. She sat for a moment thinking before she answered, and she saw him seem to swell in anger as he opened his lips to speak again. She cut him off.

"How dare you block a public road and hazard honest people who are about their lawful business by having your men and horses lying down in the way! Who are you to question me? I have lived here all of my life and am known to all decent people in this county. I am on lawful business on a public road in broad daylight!"

The captain's mouth moved without speaking. He was clearly not used to being talked to in this way. He swayed back as if to take a step back, but he stopped himself. Before he could get his body back over his feet, she spoke again. "Now, Captain, if you will ask your men to clear the public road and go about whatever business you have in this county, I will go about mine." She took up the whip and changed her grip on the reins.

"Do not move that vehicle! You, black man, damn you! Dismount and hold that horse!"

Cynthia Montgomery flushed a dark red and half rose from her seat. "You shall not use that language to Caesar or to me! What is your name and organization? I'll write to your commanding officer and report your careless and boorish behavior. You have endangered us, and then you have used the common language of the streets to us. I will not stand for that!"

The Yankee captain was as red as Cynthia Montgomery. He seemed to swell as her words lashed him. "You and your man will do as I say, and you will do it when I say to do it! Now, get down from that horse! And you, get out of that buggy so that we can search it, or I will have my men take you out of it."

The buggy whip cut him across the face as the last words were spoken. He flinched and staggered backward from the blow. His men surged forward. The first grabbed her by the arm, with the second pressing to catch her leg. The blast of Caesar's shotgun punctuated the struggle, and the two leading soldiers snapped backward with the force of the impact of the shot charges from a range of only three feet. The second blast from the double-barreled gun caught the captain high on his right shoulder and spun him backward and down to the ditch.

Caesar dropped the shotgun and spun his horse back the way they had come. "Miss Cynthia, grab hold of me! Let's get out of here!" She stood and was reaching for him when the first big bullet hit him from behind. He slumped forward but caught himself. As he straightened, he reached to take her hand, but two more shots hit him from close range and he toppled forward from the saddle, hitting the buggy as he slumped to the ground.

She was out of the buggy and by his side instantly. His back was covered with blood, and as she turned him she saw the terrible exit wounds in his chest. His eyes were open and he smiled at her. Then he was gone.

She felt as though a knife had been plunged into her heart. Her friend and protector for her young life was dead in the dirt of a country road. He had watched over her for as long as she could remember. His constant counsel of caution had always warned her of dangers that she did not see, and he had always been there, except when he had gone to war with her father. It was Caesar who had lifted her grievously wounded father to his horse and brought him home after the battle at Fort Donelson. It was Caesar and Scipio who had run the plantation while her father mended slowly from his wounds.

The furor in the road around her brought her back from her grief, and Caesar did her one last service as she slipped the big army colt from his dead body and concealed it under her skirts. Rough hands pulled her erect and spun her around to face a white-faced lieutenant.

"Get her on that horse! Put the captain in the buggy with the injured men! We need to find a doctor. Sergeant, have a corporal bring the bodies of the dead along behind us for burial in the next town. Prepare to mount! Mount! Company! Forward: March!"

Chapter 7

Albert Goddard felt a bit better this morning. He had been home for weeks and no one had bothered him. Patrols from both armies had passed through the town without taking any notice of him or disturbing the peace of the countryside. He felt as if things were getting back to normal. He looked up from his desk at the bank and savored the bright sunshine that flooded the street outside. He rearranged the papers on his desk with satisfaction. Despite his arrest and detention and the threats of Colonel Anson Grimes, he still had his property and the wealth that he had built up so energetically. Nevertheless, he was a prudent man above all else. He took very seriously the threats made by the overbearing officer. He was arranging to transfer all of his possessions to his wife. Once everything was legally put under her hand, it would be safe from the greedy hands of the profiteer. He had it all ready to sign over tomorrow when Lawyer Springer was scheduled to visit. He wrapped the pile of documents and deeds in brown paper and sealed it from prying eyes. All that would be needed now were the signatures to safeguard his hard work and sharp dealing.

A shadow darkened the window at the front of the bank. Ed Barton had stopped in front of the window and turned to gaze back along the main road. Goddard watched his motionless figure as it gazed intently at some distant sight. It occurred to him that motionless was a pretty apt description of Ed, and he smiled at his own wit. "Well, some people are smarter and more energetic than others," he reflected with the utmost self-satisfaction.

Finally, Ed turned and looked into the bank, "Morning, Mr. Goddard."

"Morning, Ed."

"There's some soldiers comin' into town, Mr. Goddard."

"Whose soldiers, Ed?"

"Our soldiers, Mr. Goddard."

Albert Goddard almost shouted in frustration at Ed, but his natural caution at the smell of danger asserted itself. He rose slowly and walked over to the door with as much composure as he could muster. He followed Ed's gaze and saw a column of blue-coated Union cavalry with a buggy and a wagon entering town at a walk. The word that leapt to his mind at the sight of the column was fatigue. They looked worn out. Horses' heads drooped, and men's heads nodded and swayed with the walking rhythm of their mounts. As the column came even with the bank building, he could see injured men in bloody bandages in the wagon and the buggy.

The lieutenant in charge of the column called his sergeant to the front and gave instructions to move the men to the edge of town across the bridge and to water the horses and rest the men. The vehicles with the wounded and the prisoner were to be moved to the shade along the street while he asked for a doctor. Albert Goddard overheard the remarks and relaxed as the lieutenant saw him and turned his horse toward the bank.

Albert Goddard slipped on his coat and stepped to the door to meet the officer. He saw a tall, fit young man with the hollow eyes and sunken cheeks of exhaustion. He heard the young man introduce himself and ask for a doctor for his wounded captain and injured men. He listened to the answers to his questions about the seriousness of the wounds and injuries, and he told the officer that he would send someone to Ridley to fetch the doctor while the wounded men and the soldiers rested here. He called to Ed Barton to race to Ridley and bring back Dr. Schubert immediately. He then offered his own home for the wounded captain until the doctor should arrive.

The lieutenant gratefully accepted the offer of such a haven coupled with some relief from his own burdens. He visibly sagged in the saddle with relief as he accepted it. Goddard instructed the soldier driving the buggy to follow him and motioned to the lieutenant to do the same.

Within the hour, the captain was in a bed in Goddard's house being fussed over by the ever-gentle Elizabeth Goddard. The two injured enlisted men had been moved to houses in the town, and the balance of the command was setting up the camp by the river bridge. Within two hours, the doctor was attending the captain. The exhausted lieutenant turned to the problem of his prisoner.

"Do you have a jailhouse here in your town, sir?"

"Yes, we do. Why do you need one?" Albert Goddard asked, his curiosity stirred by such a request.

"We have a female prisoner who must be returned to Lexington, and she has been a trial to me for days. She is the one who did all this damage. At least, it was she and a servant with her."

"She must be a formidable woman."

"She is that, sir!"

"What sort of woman is she to be able to do so much mischief?" Goddard asked.

"To see her you would never believe her capable of such destruction. She looks a very angel," the lieutenant sighed.

"Well, things are settling down here; we can go look at the jail and you can decide if it is suitable for your prisoner."

The two walked to the jail and inspected the security of the building. After pronouncing the facility adequate for the necessary task, they walked to the encampment to see the prisoner. As they approached the camp, Albert Goddard could see the girl in profile. When they were close enough to see her clearly, he stopped in mid-stride. "My God, it's her," he blurted out.

The lieutenant, half a step ahead, turned back and asked, "It's who?"

"It's the girl who was here before!"

"When? What do you mean?" The officer was puzzled, and his curiosity was thoroughly aroused. His fatigue had melted from him. His eyes were fixed on Goddard, searching his face for clues to this mystery.

"That's the girl who came here to meet the Confederate cavalry. Her name is Mary Ready. She is John Hunt Morgan's niece."

The lieutenant's interest was intense. "What did you say her name was, again?"

"Mary Ready."

"How do you know this for sure?"

"I was introduced to her by the Rebel officer. And, I will tell you, she has a tongue like a bullwhip! She blistered him right in the public street. It was something to watch!"

As they continued their conversation, they walked closer to the seated girl. Their voices, if not their words, warned of their approach, and she turned her head to see who was approaching. When they stopped in front of her, she raised her head as if seeing them for the first time.

"Ah, Mr. Goddard! Thank heavens you have come! You are a man of substance and authority in this community. Please tell this officer to release me. I am certainly innocent of any crime. His captain has assaulted me and detained me while I was traveling on a public road on lawful business."

At the mention of the name, the lieutenant started. He called for a nearby soldier to fetch something for him from the captain's bedroll and turned his attention back to Goddard and the girl. He listened as she described the bloody affair in the road, and he was surprised at the accuracy and clarity of the description. She remembered and reminded him of actions that he had forgotten. There were, in the actions of his captain, things that he would rather forget. His recollection was interrupted by the return of the soldier with the captain's dispatch case.

He opened the leather pouch and rifled through the papers in it. He took out two broadsides and scanned them quickly. His motion brought the soldier close to receive a whispered instruction. He folded and tucked the broadsides in his pocket as the man trotted away to talk to the sergeant. In a moment, the man returned with the sergeant and three other armed troopers.

"Mr. Albert Goddard and Miss Mary Ready, or whoever you are, I arrest you both for spying against the United States of America for the Rebel Government."

Albert Goddard staggered and color left his face. He gasped,

"No! I did nothing! I am a loyal citizen. I fought for the country in the war with Mexico. You can't do this. There is some mistake!"

"Take him to the jail and lock him up. Sergeant, set a guard over him to see that he talks to no one." Turning to Cynthia Montgomery he said, "You will remain here in the camp under guard as you have so far. I will attempt to find a reliable woman from the town to help you with your needs, but you will be under guard at all times."

She sat like a marble figure looking him straight in the eye. It was not fearful or hostile, but it penetrated his inward self. For the first time he faltered. "I … I … Your privacy will be protected, but you surely will be guarded as closely as modesty allows. You will not escape me, miss."

"Thank you for that consideration," was all she said. Then, she turned away.

General Hurlburt studied the cavalry lieutenant as he listened to his report. The young man had done a very good job. He had clearly captured the two spies identified in Jimmy Michaelman's broadsides. He deserved the reward, but Hurlburt knew human nature too well to not realize that the troop captain would lay claim to part or all of it, if he survived. Perhaps the best thing to do on that score was to wait without discussing the matter until the man recovered or died of gangrene. In any case, he had the two rebels in his hands and he wanted to question them carefully.

"Thank you, Lieutenant. You have done a fine job. We will need to verify some things and question the two spies, and we may find that we need more information from you, too."

"General, about the rewards …"

"It's not time for that yet, Lieutenant."

"I just wanted to say that I thought it should go to the families of the two men who were killed. Our whole troop is from the same town, and the men all feel that way."

Hurlburt relaxed. "That's a decent thing to say. We will certainly consider it when the time comes."

After the lieutenant left, Hurlburt asked Michaelman what his plan would be for interrogation of the two prisoners. Michaelman thought a minute before answering.

"Goddard will tell us anything we want to know. The question is, can we believe it. On the way here, he talked constantly to anyone who would listen. He maintains that he is a loyal Union man. He can't name any specific thing he did except warn us of Morgan's raid on Louisville. Of course, that is why we think he is a Rebel. Why would he maintain that action as a service to us, if he knew it was a deliberate deception? He would be a fool to admit it. It would hang him. He served in the Mexican War, so he knows something about military justice. It just doesn't make sense, unless he is a brilliant agent and skillful liar. If that is true, he is throwing the girl to us as a sacrifice."

Hurlburt slapped the table. "The girl will say nothing. She is undoubtedly the Mary Ready who participated in the deception. Goddard positively identifies her. He was there. If she weren't the one, then accusing her would come back to haunt him when she produced a witness to prove that she was never present. If she can't do that, she will hang. She is certainly intelligent enough to under-stand that."

"General, I believe that we have enough to bring her before a court martial and hang her as a spy. To cement the case, we should offer Goddard a pardon in return for his testimony against the girl."

Hurlburt nodded and asked if there was anything else.

"Yes there is, General. For some reason, Anson Grimes is very reluctant to turn Goddard loose. He can't or won't explain clearly why to me. Perhaps you can get a clear reason from him. It seems to me that Goddard's willing testimony is the key to successful trial of the girl. He may be talking his head off now, but if it comes to a court martial, he may fear that he is next after her. That is a reasonable fear for him under the circumstances. You need to get Grimes to go along with us, or the whole thing becomes much more difficult."

"All right. I will talk to him today."

Chapter 8

S cipio kept the mule in a steady walk; he had to resist the urge to gallop until it dropped. He knew that before the mule's strength failed, he would be stopped by somebody and asked to account for himself. Even though he carried letters from Major Montgomery explaining his mission, any delay would cost him time that might be fatal to Cynthia Montgomery. He had to find Harry Montgomery and John McKenzie quickly.

Three days had passed since he had found Caesar's body beside the road. The tracks and sign of the body of Union cavalry told him part of the story, and the people of the town where the dead Yankee soldiers were buried gave him much of the rest of it. He had delayed only long enough to tell the major the situation and to get a reliable mount. Now he felt that he was close to Morgan's command at last, because the field hands that he had stopped to talk to periodically had seen Confederate cavalry moving along this road just yesterday.

There were few other travelers on the road. Most of the people whom he saw were local people going about the business of their lives. Farm wagons, small drives of cattle or horses, and the occasional buggy were his company. If they were coming from the other direction and seemed inclined to spend a moment talking about what they had seen along the road, he asked them questions about what was up ahead. Asking about soldiers was not unusual in this much-traveled land between two armies. Often it was wise to avoid friends as well as foes if you were driving or riding a good animal.

When he noticed a large number of tracks of shod horses

moving in one direction, he increased his pace to a trot. He maintained this pace for nearly twenty minutes, covering three miles before he saw the road blocked in front of him by a heavily loaded wagon. Two men stood beside it in a loud argument. At the sound of the mule's hoof beats, they stopped and looked at Scipio.

"Gentlemen, please let me pass. I am on an important mission."

The men said nothing, but looked intently at Scipio and the mule.

"Gentlemen, my mission is very urgent. Please let me pass."

"Where are you goin' in such a hurry?" The words grated out of the man's thin, sallow face in a surprisingly low growl.

Scipio thought carefully before he answered. "I am carrying letters and messages for men of the army," he answered.

"Which army would that be?"

This was very dangerous ground. The question asked in that manner might be innocent curiosity, or it might be a deliberate snare from which there was no escape. There might be no "right" answer.

"Why, our army, sir. At least that's what the boss always calls it."

"Well, we are going to the army too, and we need your mule to help pull this wagon, so I don't guess you'll mind helpin' us out for the cause, will you? Just get down right quick, and we can all travel together."

"Gentlemen, please! I would like to help right now, but I been told to not slow down for a minute. It is very important. I must go past you. I will send back some help for you as soon as I get to the camp."

"You get down off of that mule right now! That's the only thing that's going to happen right now! Who do you think you are? Hear that, Charley? He goin' to send us back some help like he was a damned general or somethin'."

The man called Charley shook the stick that he held in his hand at Scipio as he stepped toward him. "Get down, damn you!" he shouted. Both men advanced as Scipio backed the mule away. "Get him, Curtis, he's trying to run away!" The pair lunged at him. Charley swung the stick high and downward. Scipio tried to

ward off the blow with his arm but failed. The wood struck him a
glancing blow on the temple. He lurched away from the attack at
the same time as the frightened mule shied in the same direction.
The effect was to hurl Scipio into the road as a groggy heap. He
tried to rise and swing into the saddle again from the near side
of the frightened creature, but another blow struck his wrist and
made him lose his grip. He saw Curtis catch the bridle as Charley
came around the mule's rump and struck him again across the ribs.
The next blow was against the side of his leg, and he went down
hard. He was only half conscious when he was hit again on the
back of the head.

Chapter 9

"Good Morning, General." Anson Grimes was almost friendly in his manner as he entered General Hurlburt's office.

Hurlburt looked up and studied the provost marshal. This change in manner was noticeable. Grimes, at his best, was surly and abrupt. After Grimes was seated, Hurlburt began, "We need to discuss this girl Mary Ready or whoever she is. I want to insure that we convict her and hang her. We need that kind of example for these Kentuckians to stop them from constantly helping the Rebels with supplies and information.

"In order to accomplish that, I want eyewitness testimony about her activities. We can only get that from this man Goddard. I understand that you are reluctant to offer him amnesty or a pardon in exchange for his testimony. Is that correct?"

The smile faded from Anson Grimes's face as he heard these words. He shifted in his chair and leaned forward. "That is not exactly correct. I think Goddard is guiltier of helping the Rebels than she is. We know what she has done. We don't know what Goddard has done. People in his own town say that the Rebel officer said he was a 'friend to our cause.' He did not specify how. That statement is something entirely different from saying, 'He has supplied us, or he loaned us money,' or some other such thing."

"The Rebel would hardly reveal what the man's specific contribution was in front of the whole town, Colonel."

"That may be so, General, but all the girl really did was some play-acting. Goddard was the one who actually sent the deceptive message."

"True. We also got that message from two other people who you are not accusing of Rebel sympathies."

"They weren't named by a Rebel officer as Southern sympathizers. Why not? Why was Goddard out of all of these people named, General?"

Grimes went on, "What if you offer a pardon to the Rebel spymaster for the state? I had his books and records. Why were they taken from my office during the raid that freed the prisoners?

"I'm going to ask you another question, General. What will the people in Washington say when you hang a young girl? Do you think the President will be happy with the reaction to that? The newspapers will have pictures of a pretty young girl and of the hanging. Then they will add your picture too. People don't object to hanging a Rebel here and there, but they have never liked hanging women. Believe me, I know!"

Now it was Hurlburt who shifted in his chair and leaned forward. "I still want you to think about it," he added weakly.

Grimes pressed his advantage: "I caught a pretty young widow who became a widow by poisoning her husband and three other men. When the district attorney started talking about hanging, the newspapers stirred up the men of the city to a fever pitch with sketches showing her as a pretty young girl. The mayor and chief of police were threatened with loss of the next election and some other things not so legal. When the woman finally came to trial, she was found guilty of involuntary manslaughter and sent to prison for a year. Even that light sentence got the judge into trouble."

"I understand all that, Grimes. This trial will be a military court martial, not a civilian court trial. We aren't elected." Hurlburt smiled at this sally.

Grimes smiled back. "The President *is* elected."

The words hung in the air, and Hurlburt lost his smile.

"You do what you think is best, General. The provost marshal's office will support you in whatever you decide." Grimes rose to leave. "All I am trying to do is give you the benefit of my experience."

Chapter 10

John McKenzie eased his seat in the saddle as he watched his scouts clear the ridgeline ahead of the column; his company was well ahead of the brigade as the advanced guard. General Morgan's new orders to his command were to head south into Tennessee. It was certain that he had some project in mind. McKenzie's job was to make sure that the column did not run into any enemy unexpectedly. He pushed a small group of four men who paired off into two teams to cover both sides of the road ahead. They checked well ahead and were backed up by the rest of their platoon under Harry Montgomery. The other half of the company stayed with McKenzie to add further strength to the point or to meet any threat that came at them from the flank after the point had passed. Another company of the regiment followed his company with the job of securing the flanks of the column, and each succeeding unit in the column took over the task of flank protection as it advanced. At the rear of the column, a company deployed just like McKenzie's company in reverse protected the rear. Local guides assisted when they were in areas unfamiliar to the men of the command. This system allowed Morgan's cavalry to move rapidly and reasonably safely through the countryside at will. McKenzie's company of Texans was frequently assigned to this duty, and they were good at it. The men knew their tasks and cooperated smoothly in carrying them out. As a result, the command usually moved swiftly from place to place as its commander wished.

By late afternoon, they had covered many miles through rolling countryside. McKenzie watched once more from a ridgeline as his point overtook a loaded wagon pulled by two mules. One team from the point stopped to look over the wagon as the other rode on to the next ridge. After a brief inspection, one of the point men galloped back toward Harry.

"Lieutenant, we got a wagon full of grain up there. My horse practically climbed into it when he got wind of it."

"Who owns it, the drivers?"

"That's what they say, sir, but you never can tell. They are about as scruffy looking a pair as I have ever seen. One of the mules is a fine animal and the other is a broken-down abused creature. There's a black trussed up in the back of the wagon that they say is a runaway slave."

"Let's take a look."

Harry looked over the loaded wagon as he approached. The black was lying face down in the back, and his head was covered with dried blood. He stirred as the two soldiers approached and moaned, but he made no other movement. The mules stood patiently while their drivers stood in the road beside the wagon. The two men returned his appraising look sullenly with scowls. Harry ignored them and rode forward to look at the team. When he saw the big, well-turned-out mule, he gave a start. He rode around to come closer. After a thorough look at the animal, he rode back along the other side of the wagon and noted the saddle. After a brief inspection, he continued to the rear of the wagon and gently rolled the bound, bloody man over. He looked carefully at the unconscious face. Then he rode back around to face the scruffy men standing in the road.

"That's a fine looking mule. Where did you get him?"

The tall one said, "I've owned him for years."

"How about that black in the back?"

"Caught him in the woods back a ways. He tried to steal some food from us and we caught him."

"Runaway, is he?"

"Yeah. He admitted it to us after we caught him."

"Was that before or after you broke his head?" There was an edge in Harry's voice. The men picked it up.

"He tried to get away, so we had to subdue him," the tall one answered defiantly.

Harry changed his position in the saddle and turned to look back at the ridgeline. He tapped his insignia of rank and waved for someone to come forward. As he turned back, he swung up the shotgun that he carried to cover the men in the road.

"You're a damned liar!" he rapped out. "That mule and that saddle are mine, and I have known that man in the wagon all my life." His face purple with rage, he thumbed back the hammers on the shotgun.

John McKenzie rode up just as Harry leveled his weapon at the pair. "What's the matter Harry?"

"Look in the back of the wagon, John, and then see if you don't know that mule."

John McKenzie nudged his horse forward and looked at Scipio's semi-conscious face. Then he rode around the wagon and looked at the mule, as well as the saddle stored under the seat of the vehicle. Then he rode back to Harry's side.

"Well, Harry, they are guilty of highway robbery and horse stealing at least. I wonder what else they have done that we can hang them for?"

"We didn't steal nothin' from nobody! That slave stole that mule and we caught him for you. He's a runaway and a damned liar if he says anything different!" the tall one shrieked. "They're all runnin' away and stealing everything they can get their hands on now that the war has come and there are Union troops all over the place. We honest citizens ain't being protected like we should be. A man can't make an honest livin' on the roads no more."

McKenzie turned to Harry as the man paused for breath and said, "If he says anything else, shoot him." It was a bald, laconic statement spoken quietly, but it had the desired effect.

By nightfall, the column had moved many more miles. A doctor had looked over Scipio and pronounced him sound except for a concussion and a bad cut and bruise on his head. A soldier was detailed to keep him awake and to keep cool compresses on his head until he managed to recover consciousness. General Morgan came by to look at Scipio before the trial of the two wagoners began. It was short. Testimony was given as to the ownership of the mule and saddle as well as Scipio's status as a freeman. The sullen wagoners made their case worse by persisting in their obvious lies, and they were sentenced to be hanged in the morning. The sentence was carried out duly at first light. Since there were no claimants for the wagon and the feed that it carried, it was confiscated and turned to the service of the Confederate government. Thirty minutes after first light, the column was moving south.

By the end of the second day, Scipio was coherent and able to confide his terrible message to Harry and John. They discussed the possibilities throughout the day and, after a short conference with Scipio, they went to see the general. He listened attentively to their plan and their plea before lapsing into silence. Each man stood silent, motionless, waiting. The firelight caressed the contours of each face, its flickering light imparting mobility and motion that matched the activity of the minds behind the still countenances.

Finally, John Hunt Morgan lifted his face and looked at John and Harry. He motioned to Scipio to come forward into the firelight to hear what he had to say. "It would be surely ungracious to abandon one who has helped us in our cause. We cannot do that. We must attempt to rescue this gallant lady from her distress. I cannot, however, disregard the orders and the compelling need to continue moving with my command to rejoin General Bragg in Tennessee. I cannot spare both of my best outpost officers while the command is in country that is at least under the influence of the enemy. You have advanced a plan that is feasible and may work. I will give you three of your Texans, John, and I will get a message to our contact in Lexington to assist you in whatever manner you require. Scipio is not attached to this command, so he may go with you or he may stay with Harry as he chooses. I know you want Harry in your plan, but that is not possible. I cannot lose the services of both of you."

A look of agony contorted Harry's face. He stood silent but swaying like a pine beset by a whirlwind. Scipio stepped to Harry's side and put his arm through Harry's. In the firelight, Harry's face was yellow, and his red hair washed to white in the light. Scipio could see the major lying on the litter, racked with the pain of his wounds as he arrived home after Fort Donelson, in Harry's young-old face.

John drew himself to attention and said, "Thank you, General. She will be rescued."

Morgan gave a slow nod to acknowledge the full meaning of that assertion and added, "There is one more condition to your release. You must return to this command in fourteen days without fail, regardless of your success or failure to complete the rescue."

There was no bravado in his tone when John McKenzie said quietly, "She will be safe and I will be back on time, General." He saluted and left the tent with Harry and Scipio on his heels.

Chapter 11

Cynthia Montgomery was kept locked in an upstairs bedroom of a large house that had been commandeered by the Federal army for some senior officers. A hard-faced woman of great determination was with her constantly. Her meals were brought to her on a tray, so her only time out of this confinement was when she was taken to the courthouse for interrogation. Her steadfast refusal to say anything at all to any of the several officers who questioned her, beyond stating that she was a law-abiding citizen and had done nothing wrong, had finally caused a cessation in the questioning. They still were not sure of her name and had listed her as Miss Mary Ready on the records. They warned her repeatedly that she was to be tried as a spy, and they coupled that warning with pleadings, demands, and commands that she must reveal who were the other Confederate agents in her plot. Her stony silence frustrated their every assay to trap her.

Hurlburt and Jimmy Michaelman decided to go ahead with the trial in the hope that the awesome proceeding would be enough to frighten the young woman into a confession to save her life. They were only too sensitive to the fact that they had little more evidence that she was a spy than the word of a small town banker whose reputation in his own community was that of an opportunist and exploiter. The reality was that the case amounted to the unsupported word of this man about a conversation between this girl and a Confederate officer that he reported, but which conversation turned out to be arrant nonsense that bore no relation to the actual movements of the enemy. A moderately bright defense would highlight all of this. That could leave them looking like ogres or fools or both. They were also sensitive to Anson Grimes's warnings about such a trial arousing the protective instincts of the local male population and the subsequent bad situation that might develop if they actually hanged her. Nevertheless, she had been arrested with much fanfare and public notice. To do nothing would leave them looking derelict in protecting the Republic against the stain of rebellion.

General Hurlburt felt himself wishing that the girl had never been caught. He even wished that she would denounce Goddard the banker as a Rebel agent. There was that curious side light to the reported conversation that indicated that the Rebel officer had referred to Goddard as a "friend of our cause." If she would only answer a few questions, he could make enough of whatever she said to arrest Goddard and let her go for her services to the army. But the damned girl would say nothing at all, and everybody knew it.

The trial was due to start in a few days. It would all be resolved in a week or two.

Cynthia had held to the policy of saying nothing for so long that it now came naturally to her. She broke her silence only to express her fundamental needs and acted as though her jailer were not present. She looked out of the window and noticed the guards in the back yard and at the side of the house. She observed the duration of their time on post and the frequency and hour of the change. She got to know them by sight and carefully noted the careless and the attentive among them. She finally had a private moment to better conceal the colt army revolver that she had taken from Caesar in the road. She hung it from a lace inside her voluminous skirts in front of her body so that it would not thump when she sat down.

At last, the Yankees stopped trying to get her to say anything. She was left with the sure knowledge that they would put her on trial. She still had hope that she would be missed and that a rescue would come to save her. She knew the chance of rescue was poor. She could see the guards and knew the town well enough to realize that she was near the center of a large military force. No one could force a way in and hope to get back out again. After two days, despair became her constant companion.

On the morning of the tenth day, she heard a familiar voice and song at the back of the house. She was careful to show no sign of recognition, but she wanted confirmation. She rose from her seat and took a glass of water from the pitcher and tray across the room. She went to the side windows and glanced out, then turned and did the same at the rear windows and immediately resumed her seat. It was enough. The well-loved voice belonged to Scipio. He could be heard greeting the house servants and talking about being free until he had their attention and empathy. His voice dropped then and she heard no more, but she knew something was afoot.

That evening she heard him in the hall outside her room, sweeping and straightening furniture. When her jailer opened the door and handed Scipio her tray to carry back to the kitchen, she felt a rising glow of real hope. As the woman's back was to her, she touched the butt of the big pistol and looked longingly at the back of the big woman's head. Cool reason stopped her as she realized that she had to get a lot farther than the hallway outside her door to escape to safety. Her sleep that night was fitful and anxious.

Morning brought the sound of Scipio humming as he delivered her breakfast tray. He marched right into the room when the jailer opened the door. When she blocked his path, he said, "Let me put this down, miss, and I will be right back with your tray. We got some good hot coffee and cake for you." He set the tray on a table close to Cynthia and, without glancing at her, rearranged a small bouquet of flowers wrapped in paper on her tray. He walked out of the room, and when the woman turned to let him out and lock the door behind him, Cynthia pulled the tray to her and began to rearrange everything on it. She felt the paper wrapping on the flowers. It was too thick for a single piece of paper at the bottom. When Scipio came back to the door and distracted the jailer, she pulled all of the paper from the bouquet and slipped the small piece of writing paper into the waist of her skirt. She rose and walked to the table and placed the flowers in a vase and filled the vase from the water pitcher. She handed the nearly empty pitcher to Scipio without a word and sat down to eat her breakfast.

Later in the day, when the jailer was looking out the window and Cynthia was reading, she slipped the note from her waistband and read it surreptitiously. The note was a single line:

"After first day of trial, go to school privy immediately. Knock out your guard. Change clothes."

That was all.

After supper, an officer came to the room where she was held prisoner and read the charges to Cynthia. She sat in stony silence as he read about spying and the murder of a Union officer, conspiracy to commit espionage, and assault on a federal officer. He told her that a defense counsel had been appointed for her and that he would meet her at the trial in the morning when the trial began. When this last statement was read, she laughed, and the young officer flushed scarlet in embarrassment at the obvious injustice of what he had just read. Other than the laugh, she kept silent when he asked if she had any questions.

During the night, she decided how she could secure the pistol so that it was still concealed but could be easily pulled free of her skirts. Lying in bed, she tried out her scheme two or three times before the result satisfied her, and she drifted off to sleep.

Although the school building used for the trial was only a short distance away from the house where she was imprisoned, there was an army ambulance and a small infantry escort to the school. When they arrived at the school, she hesitated a moment to find the privy. She saw what she thought was the privy to the rear of the lot near the alley behind all of the buildings, but there were several Union cavalry men around it banging away with hammers. The building seemed to be half demolished. Her hopes plunged. Her mind raced to understand what she must do, but she could find no answer.

The trial was to be held in a large room in the courthouse. She was escorted to a chair at a table facing another long table at which seven senior officers sat. The man appointed as her counsel introduced himself quickly and told her that he would do the best he could for her and that the promise included helping her after the trial. It was all that he had time for, as a gray-headed man sitting at the center of the long table called the court to order and began the proceedings.

As the morning progressed, the government presented its case. Albert Goddard told of the conversation that he had overheard. Some officers told of the Union army movement out of town that had allowed Morgan's Confederate raiders to release other Confederate spies held in the jail and to capture large quantities of stores and equipment. The lieutenant from the cavalry company told of the collision in the road and the death of two men and of the mortal wounding of his captain. He was honest enough to blurt out that it was the black servant who actually fired the shots and had been shot down in return.

It all would have been very prosaic and a bit dull if her life had not been in the balance. Nevertheless, her mind wandered and she began to look around the room. She watched as a servant brought in a pitcher of water and glasses for the court. He came back and delivered the same refreshment to the table of the prosecutor. When he came back with a tray for the defense, she almost gave a start when she recognized Scipio. Wordlessly, he put down the tray and collected the oil lamps from the courtroom and took them back to the rear of the building. At noon, the court recessed for lunch and she was taken back to her confinement. She noted that work was still going on at the privy as she left and when she returned.

In the afternoon session, she saw no more of Scipio and began to worry that she had missed the meaning of the instruction that she had been given. Should she have tried to go at noon? Did Scipio's absence now mean that the plan had failed? She lost the train of what had been said and found it difficult to come back to the present. In the end, the hopelessness of her situation brought her back to the literal content of the instructions, "After the first day of trial..." She decided to accept that and turned her thoughts to the means to get herself to the privy.

It was past mid afternoon when the president of the court finally decided to stop the trial for the day. The prosecution admitted that he was nearly complete in his presentation, but he added that he had more than an hour of presentation and summation left to go. With that, the president of the court adjourned without the courtesy of a mere nod to the defense. All rose and let the court walk out of the courtroom, and then the matron took Cynthia by the arm and steered her toward the front door.

Chapter 12

As soon as Cynthia and her jailer descended the steps, Cynthia clutched her stomach and let out a gasp and a moan. The matron released her arm and bent to look into her face. Instantly, Cynthia said the word, "Privy!" and spun around as if looking for that building. "This way!" a voice shouted, and Cynthia ran toward the privy. The matron huffed behind her but lost ground. A familiar face held open the door for both women and then closed it firmly behind them. The extra two steps of lead gave Cynthia time to extract the big colt from her skirt and grip it firmly in her skirt folds unseen. When the matron entered behind her, Cynthia turned and commanded, "Look away!"

The big woman hesitated and turned as she saw her charge fumbling with the waist of her skirt. As soon as the broad back was turned, Cynthia hit her with the pistol at the base of her skull as hard as she could. Cynthia hit her two more times to make sure that she was out for good and then looked frantically around. She saw clothes and a big straw hat for a young boy hanging at the far end of the privy. Quickly, she began to peel off the voluminous clothes that she wore and change them for the light shirt and trousers. She was no more than halfway through the change when she heard Scipio's voice cry "Fire! Fire! Fire!" She heard a great whoosh of air and flame from the back of the school building, and other voices took up the cry.

At that instant, a panel in the back of the privy opened, and John McKenzie's face appeared. "Hurry!" he said, "Hurry!"

"There are no shoes," she said.

"Don't need them," he answered and dragged her out through the panel. As he turned to slip it back into place, another hand took her by the arm and thrust a fishing pole and can of worms into her hand. She was pulled back across the alley where she and her escort stood still and watched the excitement.

John McKenzie, dressed in a Yankee sergeant's uniform, shouted, "We'll get the fire brigade! Detail, Mount!" The other three troopers with him scrambled to their horses and thundered down the alley.

When McKenzie and his men were clear of the end of the alley, 'Chilles Wallace told Cynthia, "Come on, Tommy. Let's go fishing."

They strolled down the alley and walked two blocks down toward the river before 'Chilles stopped and ducked into a rundown stable.

"Are we going to hide here?" Cynthia asked.

"No, miss. We do have to make a minor change in your disguise though. Please do not think me improper, but you are not a convincing boy in that shirt. In fact, you are quite obviously a girl." He flushed red when he said these words. She paused for a moment and then said, "Keep watch while I do something about it." She slipped into a stall and removed the shirt and her undergarments. She tore the undergarments into strips and bound them tightly around her breasts before slipping the shirt on again.

"Much better!" he said, as he led the way on down the street to the river.

They fished near a Union bridge guard for about half an hour and then walked up to the bridge, crossed at a ford below it, and fished the other side of the stream for a while until the guards lost interest in them. Only one mounted patrol had thundered across the bridge when they left the riverbank.

"We have got to hurry now, miss. There will be lots more patrols shortly. As long as we can stay ahead of them, we will be pretty safe." They hurried on across open fields to a wooded rise about a mile back from the river. In the woods were two saddled horses. 'Chilles tightened the girths, put the bits in the horses' mouths, and they swung out of the woods and onto the road headed south at a fast trot. For two full hours they kept up the pace, alternating walking and trotting until they had covered nearly fifteen miles. They came to a fork in the road with a small wooded rise between the two roads exiting from the intersection and open ground all around. It was twilight, and 'Chilles took the right fork until they were past the rise. Then they turned back into the woods and climbed the hill.

A dark form detached itself from the shadows and told them to ride on up. Then the form faded from view into the darkness without seeming to move.

At the top of the hill was a saucer-shaped depression, and a tiny fire burned under a coffee pot. Figures rose and came to greet the riders as they came into the flickering light of the fire.

John McKenzie reached up and caught her and pulled her from the saddle into his arms. Time stopped for them both, and the others waited only a moment before they went about their tasks.

"Thank God, you are safe! Oh, thank God!"

She pressed into his arms and wanted to be held like this forever. The rough wool of his gray jacket felt like the finest silk to her, and the power of his arms was as a protecting fortress. "I love you," he said and kissed her for a very long time.

In a while, they knew they had to end their private moments, and they came to the fireside with many sweet phrases echoing in their ears. He gave instructions to all to prepare to get back on the road. He explained that it was no longer safe for her to remain in reach of the Union army, so she must go to a place of safety. Scipio would take her to John's mother's home in Texas. He gave her a safe conduct and order from General Morgan that commanded that any Confederate unit should give her protection and any assistance that she might require to carry out a confidential mission on General Morgan's orders. John stressed the importance of getting into the deep South as quickly as possible and then west across the Mississippi from there. Another packet held detailed directions about a route to take. He stressed that the order from Morgan would convict her out of hand of the exact accusation that the Yankees had made if it fell into their hands. Finally, he gave her five hundred dollars in gold from his money belt. They could stay with his patrol until they got south of the Cumberland River unless they hit a Yankee patrol. In that case, his troops would attack, and it was up to Cynthia and Scipio to break contact and make their way onward on the journey without any escort.

Book Two

Flight into Egypt

Chapter 1

It took several weeks to make the journey across the Cumberland River and into East Tennessee. Cynthia and Scipio limited their travel to back roads when they could and were careful to attract no attention. They loaded the wagon with hay and wore the clothes of country people. Scipio rode at the back of the wagon, keeping a watch to the rear, and Cynthia drove the mules. At each rise in the road, they would pause before the crest and survey the country ahead to the next rise. In this manner, they reduced the surprises that they faced. Only the rising ground before the next ridgeline shortened their reaction time to strangers. At nights they camped a safe distance away from the road with fires out well before twilight. In this manner, they progressed steadily southward without problems.

At the end of the fourth week, the calm was shattered by gunfire approaching rapidly from the south. As they reached the halfway mark up the face of the ridge, a troop of Union cavalry thundered over the crest, dismounted in a storm of dust and flying dirt clods, and spread out along the ridge crest facing and firing in the direction that they had come from. Three blue soldiers reeled in their saddles and slipped to the ground or fell as soon as their horses came to a stand. The horse holders dragged the struggling, excited horses to the rear, and then some men left their firing positions and came to the wounded men to see if they could help.

The firing slowly declined as the sides settled into position and began to plan the next move. The Union captain came back to see about his wounded soldiers. He saw the wagon down slope and sent a soldier to bring it forward. When Cynthia braked at his side, he ordered some of the hay thrown out of the wagon to make room for his soldiers. That done, he turned to Cynthia and ordered her to turn around and take his men back to his base. Before he could finish his instructions, Cynthia spoke. "Captain these men are badly hurt, as you can see. They need help as soon as they can get it or they may die. There is a hospital in Chattanooga only a day and a half away. Your hospitals are at least three days north of here, even if your lines are closer. Let me carry your men on to Chattanooga. I promise I will do everything I can to get them there alive and see that they go to the hospital there."

He shook his head. "They would be prisoners that way; no!"

Her voice was soft, "Is that worse than dead, Captain?"

He was very tired, and he plainly cared about his men. He shook his head two or three times and walked over to the wounded. He squatted in the dirt beside them and told them what he was going to do. They nodded and thanked him. He rose and came back to the side of the wagon as the horse holders lifted the injured men into the nests made in the hay. "Miss, you wait here while we talk to the Rebs and see what we can work out." He called a lieutenant to him and the man rode slowly to the ridge crest with a white handkerchief tied to the guidon staff. There was a whoop faintly heard when the white flag was recognized. Cynthia was sure that she heard a high-pitched voice call out, "Wooohaaa! The Yanks are surrendering!"

The officer rode forward at a walk until a small man in butternut with a big hat rode out to meet him. Cynthia watched as the two talked quietly. After some gestures, head shaking, and nods, the Confederate rode back to his lines while the blue lieutenant waited. Soon, a shout from the Rebel officer rang across the vale between. "Bring them across, Yank, we will take good care of them."

As they watched the cartel come back to the lines, Cynthia asked the captain, "Will you give me a written safe conduct so that I can come back through the lines safely, Captain?"

He looked at her blankly. "Is that all you want?" he asked.

"If you could spare some food and a little coffee for your men for tonight and in the morning, it might help them along. Also give us their canteens for water on the road."

"You shall have all of that. Bless you! I will refrain from asking which side you are on."

"I shall be caring for your men. If they have men hurt, I will care for them, too."

In a few moments, the wagon was in motion headed south across the valley. When it crossed the crest of the ridge, the small man in butternut met the wagon and held up his hand to halt it. Cynthia reined in. "Do you have more room, miss?" he asked.

"Yes; how many do you have?"

"One hurt pretty bad, and one not so bad, miss."

"Put them in and give me some food and water for them. I also should have a pass or safe conduct so that no one will bother us and delay us in getting to Chattanooga."

Within minutes, they were on their way. Scipio stretched blankets as best he could to keep the sun off the upturned faces of the suffering men. They were quiet at first, until the numbing impact of the bullet faded, and then the pain rose and the *Via Dolorosa* began. They were stopped only once by a patrol, but the Confederate officer's safe conduct assured their uninterrupted travel. In Chattanooga, it took an hour to find the hospital, and no one paid any attention when they rolled into the yard. In a moment, Cynthia was out of the wagon seat. She grabbed the first attendant she saw and ordered him to get outside and get the wounded men out of the wagon. When he started to ask who she was to order him around, she unleashed her anger, and he scuttled out to lift the wounded into the hospital. In minutes, they were all inside, and a gray-headed doctor was checking each to see how he fared.

It was dark when the doctor finished his work on the wounded. As he finished each one, Cynthia Montgomery walked beside the litter as the man was taken to a place in the ward. She saw to it that the straw was fresh and clean in the mattress and that the man was covered and as comfortable as she could make him. She gave water to soothe dry mouths, and cool cloths to fevered and shocked faces. The other patients watched her ministrations quietly for a while.

Then, soft voices would ask for a drink or some little attention. She responded always with a smile and an answer to the request.

When all was quiet, the old doctor asked her to come and sit down in his office. He got directly to the point. "I will not beat around the bush, miss. I do not know who you are or where you come from. I do know that you have a touch with these injured men of which I have never seen the equal. If you will stay on here and continue to work doing the same thing that you did today, I—that is, we, because the two other doctors agree with me—will see that you are paid, protected, and honored as long as you stay with us and beyond. What say you? Please stay."

Her eyes filled with tears. "You do not know who I am or what kind of person I am. Why do you honor me so?"

The doctor took off his spectacles and wiped them with a soiled handkerchief. "In answer to your first statement, we do not care who you are or what your name is. We do know what kind of person you are. We watched you in a situation that most ladies of your breeding could not have handled. You are plainly a lady born and bred, and you are a courageous and kind one, of the highest and best order. Finally, we need you. These men need you. Some of them have been nearly destroyed physically by their wounds. The medical treatment that we had to give them to save their lives has often added obstacles to their recovery. They need care and kindness administered with a firm hand. You can do it."

He looked her straight in the eye and fell silent.

She dropped her eyes to her clenched hands in her lap and was silent a long time. The silence endured for several minutes, until she raised her head and returned his quiet scrutiny.

"I must tell you something," she began, "and I must ask you to not repeat it. It could mean my life if what I tell you becomes known to others. If you promise me that you will reveal nothing, I will be bound by your decision as to my working here as you have asked—or leaving immediately. The decision will be yours."

"I understand from what you have said that you will stay and work with us if I say we want you in spite of whatever you are going to tell me. Is that correct?" His voice was soft as he leaned forward to listen.

"Yes, that is correct."

"I agree to your conditions. Your private matter will remain so, whatever you decide to do." He rose and closed the door to his small office and sat down again to listen.

She told him everything. Sometimes tears filled her eyes from grief and loss, sometimes from anger and joy. She told him of her capture and the threat of death. She told him of the escape and even the brief moment in John's arms. She told him of the journey before her, and she told him of her ultimate destination. When she had finished, she was spent.

He reached out and took her hands in his own. "My dear, you are welcome to the Chattanooga Army Hospital. Your secret is safe, and you may continue your odyssey when you feel it is time. By the way, I was the one who patched up your father so that he could make his way home. You are Homer Montgomery's daughter, and my judgment of you as highly courageous was on the mark exactly. You are welcome here.

"Turning to the practical, your man can sleep tonight in the wagon. He has parked it out back. I have had my room cleared for you. I will bunk with one of the other doctors. In the morning, we hope that you will join us for breakfast at eight after the morning rounds that start at six. After breakfast, we will discuss your duties, compensation, and maintenance. Good night, my dear. My room, that is your room, is the last on the right at the end of this hall."

In the dim twilight of morning, Cynthia woke with a start to see a figure standing over her. For a moment, her heart strained as though it would tear itself out of her breast. The dark presence spoke, "I brought you some hot water to wash in, and a little tea." Cynthia shook the sleep from her eyes and sat up. The woman knelt beside her cot and handed her a hot, wet cloth. Cynthia placed the cloth over her face and inhaled the warm moist air as she laved her skin. "Where's yo' brush?" the woman spoke.

"It is in the box by the wall. Tell me your name."

"I'm Callista. I work in the kitchen. I saw what you done yesterday, an' I like that. I'm going to work for you from now on."

"No. Callista. That can't be unless the doctors agree to it." The woman regarded her silently for a very long moment. Cynthia studied this determined woman in return. She was tall and slender, not willowy. There was a certain latent power in her carriage and body. Her skin was a rich chocolate, smooth and firm. Her hair was pulled back tightly from her face. The voice was calm and well modulated. Cynthia guessed her age at about forty. Finally, Callista spoke: "If you ask them, they'll agree. You need me. You know what you want, but I know where to get it."

The logic of it made sense. "All right. I will speak to them this morning. Do you know how to help me dress?"

"Course I do."

After morning rounds, Cynthia sat at the table with the three doctors. She brought up the idea of Callista helping, after explaining the startling events of the morning. The doctors looked bemused. "Well, miss, you already have another conquest. Callista is a very strong personality. She has worked well in the kitchen as a cook sometimes and doing other tasks at other times. Last night, as you were working, she watched you for a while as you helped the patients and then started bringing to you things you needed in order to see to their needs. She seemed to know what you wanted before you asked for it. It was quite an interesting ballet. In fact, it was so smooth that you never noticed that she was anticipating you. We are willing to let her work with you, if the pair of you continue to function together so smoothly. If there is a problem, we will move her back to the kitchen."

Chapter 2

Through the fall and winter, Cynthia worked at the hospital, arranging, cleaning, and encouraging. She gave the hurt and nearly destroyed men the courage and hope of life. Because she demanded it, the hospital staff took pride in the neatness and cleanliness of the wards. Women in the community were encouraged to visit and bring small things to speed the recovery of the wounded. The respect and deference shown her by the staff and patients was extraordinary. They recognized that she was giving unstintingly to them and asked nothing for herself. A letter written for this man, a long night's vigil beside the cot of some dying lad from the country far from home, and the sight of her tears when one of her boys was lost brought to her respect that amounted to reverence.

Callista was Cynthia's shadow. Moving, anticipating, supplying, she was ever present. She slept across the door to Cynthia's room in the hallway until Cynthia found her there one night when she was awakened by cries from the ward. After the man in distress was calmed by their touch, they went back to the room.

"Callista, why were you sleeping at my door? You should have told me that you had no place to sleep."

"I got a place to sleep, but I belong there, where I can help you if you need it and keep anybody from bothering you."

"No one has bothered me."

"That don' mean nothin'. Anybody can walk in here from the street."

"But how would you stop someone?"

"Never mind. I can do it."

"I believe you can."

Thereafter, Callista slept on a pallet in Cynthia's room.

Scipio worked about the hospital, and he used the mule and wagon to haul loads for hire to make some extra money. He learned much about the course of the war by listening to the messengers who served the city headquarters. He did not like what he heard. It made him sick to hear of the advances of the Union blue. His head hurt often. Sometimes it was just a dull pain. Other times it was a blinding band of steel crushing his skull. He hid the problem from everyone for a while, but at last one of the bad ones hit him in the midst of a workday at the hospital. He collapsed to his knees in a ward, holding his head and moaning in agony. Callista called for Cynthia at the top of her lungs and ran to him. As Cynthia hurried to answer the cry of distress, Callista half carried him to the surgery, where the doctors examined him. The old doctor touched and pressed the skull around the scars on the side and back of Scipio's head. His diagnosis was hematoma of the brain. The other doctors agreed. Cynthia asked, "What does that mean?"

"He is bleeding inside his skull. If we do not open the skull, the bleeding will increase the pressure on his brain until he dies."

"Can you do that without killing him?"

"Yes, it is done successfully many times. Sometimes it is too late; sometimes there are other complications. Sometimes it works, but later the bleeding starts again inside the brain where we cannot go. We will not know until later."

She clasped her hands before her and closed her eyes. Every eye was on her as she stood silent. At last, she looked at Callista and saw something that she had not seen before. She nodded and said, "It must be done."

Scipio's recovery was slow. Although the operation seemed to relieve the pressure and give him relief, he responded as if in a dream. Callista nursed him and helped him do everything in addition to carrying out her own duties with Cynthia. As time went by, he seemed to slowly improve. The old doctor asked Cynthia to come into his tiny office at a quiet moment. She sat and looked him straight in the eye. "He's not doing well, is he?"

"He has recovered. He does not seem to have lost any mental

capacity, although his reactions seem a bit slower than they were before. Do you agree with that description of his condition?"

"Yes, it is true. May I call Callista in to hear this, too? She has an interest as strong as mine."

Callista came in and knelt by Cynthia's chair. Her face was taut and intense.

"Why has he not recovered all the way?"

"We do not know. Head injuries are a mystery to us in many ways. The blows that he received might have killed another man. From what I know of him and of you, the only thing that saved his life was his will to save yours. He must have been in gradually increasing pain for some time. He has resisted giving in to it because he feels responsible to get you to Texas. We have relieved him of the pain, but I must tell you that I do not know if we have relieved him of the injury. The bleeding may start again. If it does start again, it will probably be fatal.

"I am going to give you a medical opinion. You may act on it or not as you choose. If you take my advice it will not be to my benefit, and in the end, it may not be to yours either."

She said only, "Yes, go ahead."

"If you continue here, he will feel the stress of not doing what he has promised to do. It may bring on another fatal bleeding session as his apprehension grows. Anything could bring it on. Picking up a litter. Bending over to get into bed. Anger. Joy. Almost anything that would stress or excite him more than usual can bring on more bleeding. If you go on your journey, the stress of anxiety will be gone, but the danger of overexertion or some crisis on the road may do the same thing. At least if that happens, he will have the satisfaction that he gave the last measure of devotion to your father, to your fiancé, and, most of all, to you. Men have been content to die for less, and few will have died as selflessly if that becomes the case. On the other hand, if you do make it to Texas and he can rest after his ordeal, he may live many years."

The dam of restraint broke, and Callista gave a great sob and fell to the floor. "Don't take him away from me! Please don't take him away from me! I can't go with you if you leave. My master will not let me leave!"

Cynthia was speechless. She had not thought about this problem even though she had observed the bond growing between Scipio and Callista. "Come, Callista, no decision has been made, yet. Let me talk to the doctor and see what else we can do. Go and wash your face and see how our boys are doing while I find out more."

There was a flicker of hope in Callista's eyes as she looked at Cynthia. Her control came back and she silently left the room.

Cynthia sat with head bowed for a few long seconds and asked the inevitable question. "Who owns her?"

"She is owned by a Mr. Rath. He is a hard man and rents her labor to the hospital."

Cynthia thought for a moment. "Are there any lawyers who are honest and unaffiliated with Mr. Rath?"

The doctor smiled at the form of the question. "That is a tall order in this town with all the young men gone to war. Let me ask around discreetly."

In the end, they could find no one who satisfied Cynthia until a badly wounded captain asked Cynthia if she needed an attorney. She talked to him a bit and discovered that he had indeed been a practicing attorney before the war and was admitted to the Tennessee Bar. She got some orderlies to carry his cot outside into the sunshine and sat beside him as she told him what she wanted. After about an hour of discussion, they agreed on what she should do.

"But you cannot walk yet, Captain. How shall the negotiation be done? We cannot do it here. There is not really a private place."

"We shall do it by letter, miss. It will take a bit longer, but it makes the transaction more sterile. I should not want him to find out the emotional content of the sale."

Over the next two weeks, a flurry of letters went back and forth as the price went down slowly from $1200 Confederate to $650 for a prime female house slave of middle age and good health, skilled in hospital work. Cynthia was deadly serious about the negotiation, but the captain was thoroughly enjoying himself. "Look here, Miss Cynthia, he has come down about as far as we can get him. We have only two ways to go. We can tell him that you will not pay so much and see if he will come back to the table with his minimum offer. Or, we can offer him a low price to see if he accepts it or counters with a split-the-difference offer."

Cynthia turned the offer over in her mind for a moment and said a silent prayer for John to forgive her if he did not approve of the use of Confederate gold for such a personal purpose. "What if we offered him gold instead of Confederate scrip?"

"Ah, Miss Cynthia, you are an absolute delight as a client! Let's offer him $150 gold, take it or leave it. Can you pay that much?" he added apprehensively.

"Do you think he will take it?"

"We will see, won't we!"

For four days they heard nothing. Then they got a single sheet of paper with the words, "Done, send money and bill of sale for signature tomorrow. I won't pay the lawyer." It was signed with a scrawl, "Rath."

"Oh, dear, we did not talk about your fee at all. How much will it be?"

"Miss Cynthia, it will be a high price. I want one dollar, Confederate, and the privilege of keeping this note from Mr. Rath. I feel better than I have felt since I was wounded, and you have shown me that I am a good lawyer still. Bless you!"

"But you are not finished yet, Captain. There is one more document to prepare."

"What is that? I have already written out the contract."

"Scipio is free. His wife shall be free, too."

Chapter 3

Once the wagon was across Brown's ferry and on the road south into Alabama, Cynthia and Scipio began to relax and fall back into the habits they had established before coming to the hospital in Chattanooga. Callista was watching and learning the routine. The farewell had been difficult. All of the patients who could walk, and many who got their friends to carry them, were outside lining the road to say goodbye. The doctors presented her with a silver cup that had been engraved with the doctors' names and the hospital's name and date. There was a verse from Proverbs on the opposite side that brought tears to Cynthia's eyes: "Her sons rise up and call her blessed." At the last moment, there was a minor change to their plans. Two patients pleaded to be taken with them back to Texas.

Bobby and Lon were boys from Texas who had been wounded in the same cavalry fight. Both had survived terrible wounds against the expectations of every professional medical man who treated them. Neither was ever going to fight again, so they could go home, and they saw the chance to do something better than walk on a long hard journey. Scipio was able to find some extra rations to help with their keep, and they were given to understand that both of them were still soldiers of the Confederacy under orders to escort Cynthia to her chosen destination in Texas. When they had accomplished that task, they were to be released from service. Cynthia was given an elaborate document full of Latin that purported to make her a captain in the Provisional Army of the Confederacy. In translating the Latin as the order was read to all assembled, the doctor left out the phrase noting that the rank was honorary. The doctors felt that Cynthia had enough personal status and presence to get the men to do what she wanted, but they also felt that the concept in the minds of Bobby and Lon that she was actually an officer might do no harm and a lot of good.

From the first night on the road, they worked out camp routines and began to know each other. Bobby was from a farm south of Houston, and Lon was from Fort Worth. Both had been in Houston when the war started and had enlisted in Ben Franklin Terry's cavalry regiment. They had fought in every major engagement until they were wounded and sent to the hospital in Chattanooga. Bobby admitted that his farm was long gone for taxes, and he needed to start over again. He told Cynthia, Scipio, and Callista that he and Lon had been friends since the day of their enlistment. Before they were wounded, they had been in every fight the Rangers had made. He had been unhorsed twice in battles, and both times Lon had gone to him under heavy fire to snatch him back from capture by the advancing Yankees.

Bobby was about medium height and lean. He had a beaky nose planted between high and prominent cheekbones. His blue eyes were piercing. His features gave him an imperious look during his deep silences as he assessed a task or an approaching stranger, but his eyes squinted shut when he roared with laughter.

Lon was a bit smaller but of a heavier build. With sandy hair and brown eyes, the talkative Lon was a contrast to his largely silent friend. Despite his chatter, he was always busy inspecting, checking, and correcting things. Bobby told Cynthia privately that Lon would have been company first sergeant If he had not been wounded. He was a superb horseman. His handling of the mules was easy and confident. Lon had a small plot of ground and a carpenter shop. He and Bobby agreed in the hospital to work as partners on his farm and in his building work when they got home.

Scipio told about his life on the Montgomery property. He told funny stories about the major and about Cynthia as a child. They were the kinds of stories that all families have. He avoided anything about the war and its dislocations and grief. After his own stories, he asked questions about Texas. The Indians bothered him. He remembered the stories that his father had told him about the early days in Kentucky with the Shawnees. He said that he wanted to farm too, but he was not looking forward to having to fight to stay alive on his land.

Lon reassured him that the Indians usually stayed well north and west of Dallas. When they raided farther south, there was usually plenty of warning. He did admit to having one small brush with the Comanches when they chased him for about eighteen miles nearly to Fort Worth.

Callista did not have much to say. She said nothing about her past. Her only contribution was to say that she wanted to know all she could learn about farming.

When they were far enough south in Alabama to pick up the roads west that would take them to Vicksburg, they stopped to replenish their provisions and rest the mule. The place they chose to rest was beside a small Episcopal church at the edge of town. The rector of the church welcomed them and gave them permission to camp and to cut firewood and to use the well for water. He watched, bemused, at the military procedure they used to set up their camp. Each person had a job to do and got to it efficiently.

As they were finishing their evening meal, they heard a call from the twilight. A slight woman with gray hair identified herself as Mrs. Jones, the rector's wife. She brought them some freshly baked bread. Everyone in the party rose to receive her and greeted her with sincere thanks. She was invited to join them, and a small amount of the precious real coffee was brewed to go with the bread. She declined gracefully and bid them goodnight.

Over the next several days, they searched for and bought food and supplies. They bought three mules, a harness in order to use one of the new mules to help pull the wagon, and saddles for riding the other two. Weapons were cleaned, and one man was put on guard every night. On Sunday, all five attended church and were welcomed by the old men, women, and children who made up the congregation. One old man talked to Bobby and Lon after church. He asked them to come with him to his house. Shortly, they were back, carrying a heavy package between them.

Cynthia and Scipio watched as they put down their burden and unwrapped their canvas package. The folds of the canvas were opened to reveal a small cannon mounted in a "u" shaped frame that had a long spike projecting from the bottom of the "u."

"What is it?" Cynthia asked.

"It's called a swivel gun, miss."

"What good is it to us?"

"It is used against people, miss. There are just five of us, and one has to handle the mules on the move. That leaves two of us outside the wagon and only one besides you and Callista. We have talked to folks all along the way, and we have been warned about bummers and so-called guerrillas that rob and murder both sides when they can overpower them. With all of us shooting but the driver, we only have four shots before they close with us. Five shots if the driver gets off a pistol shot. Chances are, we would not hit more than two out of a crowd on a good day, and that will not be enough to keep them off of us."

"But how will we shoot that heavy thing?"

"Lon is a pretty good carpenter, and we got us some lumber out of a derelict house on the edge of town. He is going to build a mount that is sturdy and well braced for it, and we can try it out before we leave."

Within about three hours, Lon had a heavy timber hurdle built across the front corner of the wagon bed. Although the structure and its bracing took one corner out of the floor space of the wagon bed, it was not too much space. Lon went ahead and made Cynthia's bed a part of the bracing and put a storage locker under it for powder and shot for the swivel gun. When he told the purpose he had in mind for the locker, she paused a long time and said: "I think you do not want me to use the candle or lantern in the wagon bed anymore since you have me sleeping on a powder keg?"

"Oh, my, no miss! I, we did not mean anything like that. We just wanted to make a comfortable, sturdy bed for you, and we needed to store the powder and shot somewhere."

She laughed and said that she was only joking; she knew that she should not do that with the powder stored anywhere in the wagon bed. Relieved, they proceeded to mount the swivel and prepare a test firing. When the gun was loaded, they touched it off with a roar by a jerk on a cord attached to the flintlock firing device. When the billows of black smoke thinned, they could see a cloud of dust settling into the furrows cut by the handful of musket balls that they had loaded into the wicked little cannon's muzzle. The mounting frame had endured very well, and the effectiveness of the gun was awesome. The group enthusiastically pronounced it a great success and made up six cartridges with which to speedily load the gun. Lon fashioned a pouch out of a piece of scrap canvas to hold the cartridges and fixed it to the side of the wagon beside the gun mount. A small powder horn of their best powder was set aside to prime the piece and was slung over the breech of the gun.

Chapter 4

A cold wet spring changed to summer as they worked their way westward. The roads got worse as they moved through Alabama and Mississippi. The evidence of the movement of large bodies of troops and heavy-wheeled vehicles was everywhere. The people were no longer so open and friendly. Their farms looked run down, and livestock was scarce. Even chickens seemed to have disappeared from the farms. The little party was usually met with frozen faces and hard looks until they offered to pay for produce or poultry. Even then, the farm families were secretive about just where the things they delivered to the camp came from.

Lon, Bobby, and Scipio became tense and wary themselves and chose to move early in the morning and get off the roads in the afternoon as soon as a campsite with good water could be found well off the road. The mounting of the guard each night was a serious business, and the cumulative strain began to show on all of their faces. The two women took the first three-hour spell on guard to give the men some early rest. During the hours of darkness, they sometimes heard shouts and shots in the distance. Sometimes fires lit the sky. The sight of burned houses got more frequent as the sight of families got scarce.

After a particularly noisy night with much gunfire, they started moving before it got full light. A half an hour's travel brought them to a ruined shack at a crossroads. The litter of a sizable fight was everywhere. Equipment, bodies, and dead horses were along all of the entrances to the intersection. The shack stood about fifty yards away from the crossing on the northern road. With everyone alert and armed, Lon and Bobby quartered the field, checking the bodies for signs of life or valuable equipment. Scipio and Cynthia covered their movements with the swivel gun and a rifle while Callista managed the team. Lon went into the shack and let out a shout. Bobby followed him, and Scipio advanced to get closer for support. Lon came out and ran back to the wagon.

"Miss Cynthia, they's a Yank officer in the shack. He is alive, but he is in a bad way."

Cynthia scrambled down from the wagon seat and walked quickly to the cabin. At the door, she stopped and peered in. The light was bad, but the sallow, sweaty face of the man was clear enough to see. His feverish eyes looked unfocused toward the door, and he tried to speak but could only moan. Cynthia asked for water and some cloths from the wagon and asked Bobby and Lon to bring the man outside and put him in the shade of the trees.

She and Callista bathed his face and stripped him with Scipio's help. When the two of them had cleaned him and slaked his thirst, she and the rest agreed to find a sheltered place away from the crossroads but close by. They would camp there for the night and finish caring for the man there.

Bobby took his mule and found an accessible campsite in a wooded valley a few hundred yards up the road. Within an hour, they had moved to the site and had supper on the fire. With some broth and more water in him, the Yank gained a bit of strength and talked a little. His gratitude was touching. "They left me behind. They left me to die. Thank you, thank you for saving me." Soon he was asleep. They posted sentinels and banked the fire for the night.

The next morning the Yankee was stronger and told them a little more. He was an engineer major. He had been on a reconnaissance escorted by a troop of cavalry. He had consumption and had caught some sort of fever that brought him near death. At a peak of the fever, a group of Rebel cavalry had surprised them and thundered into their camp firing and slashing. The Union troopers had fired a few shots with whatever arms came to hand and had run off. They did not come back, and the Rebels never more than glanced at the ramshackle structure. He did not know how many days had passed since he had run out of water or been without food, as he had lost consciousness for long periods.

He continued to express his thanks. After a few days, he asked Cynthia what they were going to do with him. She thought a long time and studied him intently before she answered his question. "We don't have a plan about you. We did not expect your company. Right now we will just take care of you until we get where we want to go or we get to where you want to go."

"You won't turn me over to the Rebel army as a prisoner of war?"

"No," she said, "not unless you want us to. You must realize that if we meet a party, they can take you away from us if they want to, if the force they have is larger than ours.

"Now I have a question for you. Actually, I have several questions for you. What is your name? Where do you want to go? What will you do if we meet Union troops?"

"Fair questions all. I am Major Owen Davis of the Illinois engineers. Mostly, I just want to go home. I am dying and I know it. I would like to do that among friends. At my lowest point, the army abandoned me. I no longer feel any strong tie to them. So, yes, I just want to go home. If you have some good paper, I will write you a safe conduct to get you wherever you want to go. I am appointed as an acting assistant adjutant general on General Grant's staff, so the safe conduct will be good anywhere you go in the west.

"That brings up the question from me; where do you want to go?"

"Texas," she answered without hesitation.

There was a long silence between them. "Texas," He spoke softly. "It is a place as far away as the moon. I have always imagined it as a romantic place. Is it romantic for you?"

Cynthia paused and blushed scarlet, but her voice was firm. "Yes. It will be our new home. My fiancé lives there."

"Is he there now?"

"No, he is with the army."

"May he return safely to you." It was said quietly and firmly without affectation. She touched the back of his bony hand with the tips of her fingers and then gave it a gentle pat.

The next morning, they were on the road again early, pressing westward. Bobby and Lon alternated riding well ahead of the wagon, while Scipio watched the road behind them from the back of the wagon. Owen Davis lay on a pallet on top of two wooden chests, still too weak to do much more than sleep and eat.

For several days, they moved unmolested in this manner. Major Davis regained some strength and color with the food and rest given him. He asked to help in the rear guard duties in order to free Scipio to help Cynthia and Callista drive the heavy wagon, and he took the first watch after dark to allow Scipio, Bobby, and Lon a longer period of rest before their own time on sentry duty.

About a week later, a flood of gray riders coming from their rear overwhelmed them. The Confederate cavalry forced them to the side of the road and held them with a small guard while a long column of riders trotted past. The little party sat quietly until a trooper broke from the column and tried to force Lon to give up his mule in exchange for the man's broken-down horse. There was a very tense moment until the lash of a whip scalded the man's shoulders. He cried out in pain and wheeled to face his tormentor. Cynthia Montgomery looked him square in the eyes and said, "If you please, keep your hands off private property." He advanced on her belligerently, but she only sat down without taking her eyes off his eyes. "Call your officer at once. I wish to speak to him."

It was spoken softly but with confidence in the power of the request. He paused a moment and, without speaking, he rode back along the column to a group of horsemen beside the road watching the column pass. There was some conversation with a young officer at first, until a very large, older man interrupted. A few words passed, and the soldier pointed at the wagon a few hundred yards up the road.

The big man wheeled his mount and trotted down the road to the side of the wagon.

He made a bow from his saddle and asked, "What seems to be the trouble, miss?"

"I believe everything has already been resolved, thank you, sir. Your man sought to exchange his worn-out mount for one of our mules. I interfered, perhaps a bit too vigorously. He was kind enough to call you to resolve the matter. As we have not yet been introduced, perhaps you would be so kind as to tell me who you are, sir?"

She noticed the wreath and stars of a Confederate general officer on his coat collar as she spoke her question. He smiled and bowed again. "I beg your pardon, miss. The press of the business of war has dulled my manners. I am General Forrest. All of these men are of my command, and we need good mounts for the benefit of the country."

"Ah, General Forrest, I am Cynthia Montgomery, daughter of Colonel Homer Montgomery. I believe you know my father."

"Indeed I do, miss! He is one of the most gallant soldiers of our army. But, tell me, why are you so far from him and so close to the besieged army in Vicksburg?"

"General, if you can spare me a few minutes of your time in private conversation, I can give you some messages intended for your eyes that will explain much of what you wish to know."

Forrest gave some instructions to the party of officers gathered around him, and all but two rode on with the column. He dismounted and helped Cynthia down from the wagon seat after she had gotten the packet of papers from a chest inside the wagon. They walked a few yards away from the wagon and stopped as she handed him the safe conduct from John Hunt Morgan. When he had finished reading it, she handed him the safe conduct from the Yankee cavalry captain, the Confederate cavalry captain, and that from the hospital in Chattanooga. Finally, she handed him the new one written by Owen Davis and dated only two days ago.

"Perhaps, miss, you will explain this extraordinary collection of documents."

In five minutes, she had given him a good summary of her situation and purpose, as well as the circumstances surrounding each document.

"A remarkable story, miss. Please tell me what this mission is that you have undertaken way down here for General Morgan. He is even now pressing the enemy hard well to the north of here."

She told him of her arrest and escape and of her destination. His quick mind followed each sentence without deliberation and his response was immediate. "You have set for yourself a task of extraordinary difficulty. Vicksburg is almost surrounded. Yankee gunboats control the river above and below the town and have successfully run past the guns on the bluffs several times. The command at Vicksburg has little power to aid you.

"This Yankee safe conduct from this Major Owen Davis; is it real? Is it valid? Where did you get it?"

"It is real and valid so far as I know and he knows. I got it from him."

"How did you ever do that? Upon my soul, miss, you are a very formidable young woman. Truly you are Homer Montgomery's daughter! Where is this Major Davis that you could accomplish this so easily?"

"He is in the back of the wagon, General."

Forrest's jaw dropped in surprise. "What? What? You have a tame Yankee officer who will write you such documents at your whim?" he said incredulously. "Tommy, go get that damned Yankee out of the back of the wagon and bring him here, right now," he barked at his aide.

The young officer ran to the wagon, drawing his pistol to bring back Owen Davis. While he was on his errand, Cynthia Montgomery explained the circumstances of finding Owen Davis and his physical condition. In minutes, the staff officer was back, supporting a pallid and staggering Owen Davis.

Davis came to attention as best he could and saluted courteously; then he quickly asked leave to sit before he fell down. Forrest nodded, and the staff officer helped Davis to a nearby stump.

Forrest studied him for a long time and then shot the question, "What were you doing in this neighborhood, Major?"

"Now, General, you know very well that I must not answer such a question as your prisoner."

"You are not yet my prisoner, Major, but if you do not answer my questions, you may be very shortly—or shot as a spy." His tone of voice was level and without idle threat or bombast, but it was plain that he meant every word.

"Then, General, you must do as you see your duty. My duty precludes me from answering any such question. If you make me a prisoner, I will not be one long, as a higher power will release me in the near future. If you shoot me as a spy, you will not advance the date of my death by much. If I'm to be shot, I would rather it be as a spy than as a traitor."

Forrest stood silent considering.

"Major, I know what your corps and duty is, and I know where you were found. I expect I already know all that I need to know about you and your military mission. This young lady has told me about where she wants to go and about each member of her party. She knows all of them well except you. I am going to ask you a question that relates to your military duty, and I want an honest and complete answer. This party is trying to cross the Mississippi and get to Texas. They intend no hostile act to either side. Will you do all in your power to help them to their goal?"

Davis was silent for a long moment. Then he looked Forrest squarely in the eyes and asked, "May I speak to you privately, General?"

Chapter 5

"What did you want to tell me, Major?"

"Miss Montgomery told me a great deal about her travels, but she did not tell me all. As it happens, I know why she is making her way as far away from the Federal army as she can."

Forrest said nothing. He only continued his unblinking gaze on the feverish man before him.

"General, I was in the courtroom in Lexington on the day that she was brought before the court martial. I heard the arraignment and knew exactly what was planned. My engineers were there to build the gallows."

Forrest's face darkened with the rush of blood, and a vein on his forehead stood out like rope. His jaw clenched, he said nothing, but his anger was palpable.

"I see the enormity of this thing affects you the same way it did me. I abhor what was being planned and was joyful at her escape. Her kindness and gentle care of me when she had no obligation to render aid in the current circumstances marks her as a worthy and honorable person. She has been honest and generous to a foe. I wish to give you my personal word of honor that I will do nothing whatsoever to harm her or impede her in any way."

"She needs more from you than that, Major. She must get across the Mississippi River past the gunboats and the navy patrols. These people have no experience in crossing a river under these circumstances. They will be stopped because they are unusual; they will attract enough attention to be searched. The weapons that they hold and the character of the party will be disclosed when the various safe conducts are found.

"If you are as supportive of her escape as you say you are, you will have to use your official position to help them across the river and as far west as the Federals control, as well as through the picket line and into Confederate control. You understand what that means?"

The Yankee major grew paler as the import of what Forrest proposed came home to him. He was to use his official position to aid an escaped military prisoner who was a suspected spy. It would mean a firing squad for treason if he were caught.

"Yes, General, I understand." He paused before adding, "and I will see it through, God willing."

"See to it, and be quick about it. You do not have much time." Forrest took a few long steps and swung into the saddle. He saluted Cynthia Montgomery and galloped down the road after his command.

Two days later, they made camp late and were still closer to the road than they wanted to be. They could not find a better place close by, so they agreed to put out fires before twilight. Fires were duly out after a spare supper was finished, and the sentry was posted. Those not on duty were still awake checking their arms and priming. Blankets were rolled out and all were settling down when Scipio, who was on first sentinel, called an alert and ran back to the camp just ahead of a group of about twenty horsemen.

The group was unkempt and plainly not regular cavalry of either side. The leader reined in and slowly surveyed the camp. Scipio stood in front of him holding his shotgun. Bobby was at the rear of the wagon with his rifle leaning against the tailgate. Cynthia was inside just behind the driver's seat. The major was seated inside the wagon out of sight of the intruders but at the mounted swivel gun. Lon had gone to get a bucket of water and was coming back through the woods to the left of the group of horsemen.

"Where you folks from?" the leader growled.

Bobby spoke from the rear of the wagon. "Back east. Who are you?"

"I am Colonel Tom Fagan of the 57th Mississippi Partisan Rangers. What you got in the wagon, boy?"

"Our stuff," Bobby answered.

Bobby could see the major, hidden from the intruders' view by the wagon tarp, rise and swing the swivel gun to point at the center of the packed group of raiders. As the major quietly cocked the piece, Bobby spoke to Scipio. "Scipio, you need to help the Colonel down from his horse."

Scipio nodded and stepped forward to grab the bridle of the big horse. As he did so, the muzzle of the shotgun swung up to the man's belly, and then he fired. His shot lifted the big man from his saddle, a broken bag of bloody meat. Scipio dropped to the ground as soon as he fired. His shot was followed instantly by the roar of the swivel. A tongue of flame, smoke, and musket balls blasted through the concealing canvas and licked a swath of death and destruction through the middle of the group. Bobby and Lon both shot a man out of the saddle while the few survivors galloped screaming back to the road and away in the gathering darkness. Both men whipped out their bayonets and finished off two or three who tried to rise. Five badly maimed men lay bleeding and moaning amid the tangle of bodies in the clearing.

Cynthia rose to climb down and see to the wounded, but Owen Davis grabbed her arm and pulled her back into the wagon under its canopy. "No, miss! You must not go out there."

"I worked in a hospital. I know what wounded men look like."

"It is not the same. This is a battlefield, and such places are very different from anywhere this side of hell. I beg you; let us take care of what needs to be done. I promise, we will call you, if we think you can be of service in this task."

His face was tight and hawk like. His eyes were wide and staring. His sickly pallor was gone, and his cheeks were flushed red with pulsing blood. Bobby looked into the wagon with the same lethal tension in his face. Cynthia knew, then, the difference between battle and the rest of life for these men. The intensity of the experience and the carnage consumed humanity. Man became a killing machine.

She silently nodded and sat heavily down on her bunk as Owen

Davis climbed down from the wagon. They dragged the remains of both animal and man down into the woods. The bodies were searched for weapons, supplies, and valuables that would be of use to the party. The pickings were slim. There were two decent horses caught in the woods. The weapons were of poor quality and badly cared for at that. Some ammunition and a bit of money were salvaged. A pair of good binoculars, a blanket or two, and a pair of boots that fit Lon was the balance of the spoils of war.

Of the five who were alive when the shooting stopped, two were dead when Bobby and Lon came back from their grisly task. The other three were badly hurt and unlikely to last more than a day or two. It was decided to stay put until early dawn rather than get on the road in the dark and unknowingly ride into an ambush set by the survivors or some other band. The wounded were bandaged and made as comfortable as possible. The guard was doubled, and they endured a night of moans and sobs. No one slept much, and all were eager to get moving in the pre-dawn darkness.

As they finished loading, Scipio asked what was to be done about the wounded outlaws. "Leave them," was the comment of Bobby and Lon. Owen Davis spoke up. "We cannot do that. That is what was done to me. We will carry them on the tailgate of the wagon to the next settlement and turn them over to the sheriff if there is one."

The sun was well up when they saw a group of houses through the trees ahead. Scipio, who had been silent all morning, asked a question. "What if one of these men came from this town?"

The question exploded in their minds like the blast of the swivel gun. Only Bobby, who was riding ahead, did not hear the question or consider its implications. All of the rest stared at Owen Davis. His own pale face grew ashen. "If we go into that settlement and they see me in my uniform, they will react. They may or may not know what these men have been or done. They may not care. They may be from here. The men may be the enemies of the town, and the people may jail them or worse. We just do not know."

Lon whistled for Bobby to come back to the wagon. Bobby heard the situation and was quick to come up with an idea. He studied the three wounded men on the tailgate of the wagon and then turned to the group. "If we put them down here or in the village, the people will have a good idea that we have done them in. If we turn around and leave them to be found, it would be easy for any sheriff to follow the wagon tracks and find us. They are unconscious. If we hide them in the wagon and take them through the village then drop them off and one of us rides back and announces that we found them, then that is the only association the people of the village will have between us and the wounded men. The men are wounded and unconscious and will not know how they got there or where we have gone. They will not be able to point to us in any way until we are long on the road. This way we will do as Major Davis wishes and not simply leave them to their fate, nor will we risk ourselves too much."

Chapter 6

They began to meet more people on the roads, even though they tried to travel on the smaller back roads. The news about Vicksburg was not good. The Federals had completely surrounded the city and shut off almost all contact with the rest of the Confederacy. No supplies and no one other than the most skillful scouts could make their way into or out of the city.

A crossing under the guns of the Gibraltar of the West was out of the question. They had to decide whether to cross above the town and outside the lines of the besiegers or south of the encircling lines. Owen Davis warned them that crossing above the town would be nearly impossible because Federal outposts on the other side of the river extended well to the north to cover the lines of supply. South of town, the river was more accessible, and the only patrols were navy gunboats and small boat patrols. It was known that the Confederates had been receiving deliveries of cattle from Texas across the river south of Vicksburg. They discussed the hazards of being intercepted by the blue cavalry and worked out how to represent themselves. Owen Davis agreed to stay in the background unless Yankees caught them. With Confederates, they would rely on the safe conducts that they already had.

From this point on, they moved only in the twilight with a rider well out front. They turned south and found roads largely empty. On the third day, they met a large herd of cattle moving east escorted by a company of Confederate cavalry and some civilian drovers. Two of the flank riders converged on them, one to the front and the other behind but not on line with the lead man. "These folks know what they are doing," Bobby said softly. After a few questions and the presentation of one of the passes, the questioner rode back to the herd and to his officer. The captain and a corporal rode back and questioned them some more until he understood who they were and where they were going.

"Miss, I can't stop this herd to help you right now, although I would like to. We've got to get some distance between the Yankee cavalry and us. We will stop about three miles southeast of here for the night, and if you can follow us, you can talk to some of the drovers who brought the cattle from Texas and across the river."

A brief conference settled the matter, and they followed the cattle to a campsite on the edge of an open prairie. A slender cowboy soon appeared at their fire. Cynthia touched a somno- lent Scipio and pointed to the man's spurs. Scipio smiled, and for a moment his eye held the old spark of intelligence and wit. He spoke one word that caught the visitor's attention: "Texas."

"Yes, miss. I'm Tom. The captain said you folks wanted to cross the river and get to Texas. I have been doing that for a while now. What would you like to know?"

"We need to know where, when, and how to cross the Missis- sippi."

"Are you going to take the wagon along or leave it behind?"

"We need it. Two of us are not well, and we need to be able to carry enough provisions so that we can stay out of the way of the armies and some of the people who hang about them."

"Miss...miss, that will make it very hard. There are Yankee gunboats patrolling the river, and they have small boats full of soldiers or sailors at night that are much harder to spot, although they do not move as fast as the gunboats. You can get away from them if you can travel light. The problem is that the Yankees have captured or destroyed all boats big enough to carry your wagon. We leave our wagons on the west bank and swim our horses and cattle across."

Cynthia's face fell at this news. Her mind raced for a solution. "If there is no way to get it across, I guess we will have to leave it behind."

Owen Davis' pale face appeared from the darkness of the

wagon. "If Tom can get us to a crossing place that has an easy slope into and out of the river, I know how to get the wagon across if we can get a boat and five or six men to row us across."

All eyes focused on Tom's lean, handsome face. "That's just what we use to get the cattle in and out of the river. We have to get a move on, though. The river is low and slow now, but if there is a rain up stream, it will be very dangerous to try to get across without even considering the Yankee navy patrols. How quickly can you do what you want to do, mister, when we get to the riverbank?"

"One or two days, if there is a lot of small underbrush along the bank. The time will be shorter if we have some help."

"I have two men with me and we will help out. What else do you need?"

"A good-sized rowboat with four oars. We will need plenty of ropes, a good sound large wagon canvas, and a lot of resin."

Tom considered before answering. "I can get four ropes from the supply wagon. We can swap your tarp for theirs, since it is a little bigger. I will send my two men ahead to slash some pine trees so the resin will have a chance to run."

The major nodded, and asked, "How long will it take to get to the river bank?"

"My men can make it in a day of hard riding, barring a brush with a Yankee patrol. With luck and dry roads, the wagon can make it in two full days."

"If everybody agrees, we must start at first light." Owen Davis had a coughing spasm and lay back out of sight. The others divided up the watch for the night and immediately went to their blankets.

Chapter 7

When the wagon arrived on the riverbank at twilight, they found a small fire well back from the water shielded by a blanket strung between two trees and an enormous pile of cut brush. Davis was too weak to stand, but he directed the work from a box. Bobby and Lon and the two cowboys bundled the brush into tightly packed bundles of equal lengths. Scipio and Callista were set to coating the large tarpaulin with pine resin. Cynthia stepped in to help Scipio, too, when he began to hold his head and stare into space. Before an hour was up, he was prostrate, confused, and incoherent. He was placed gently on his blankets while his head was bathed with wet cloths cooled by spinning in the air before being put in place. His restless movement continued until just before first light. By full dawn, he was breathing hard and rattling in his throat, but his body, though tense, was still. In another hour, his breathing stopped.

After his last breath, Cynthia covered his face with his blanket. She was still for a long time. Inside, her mind was numb. She was alone. Her father was far away. There was no news from John. Caesar was dead. Scipio was dead. Everyone she knew was gone. The beloved adviser and teacher was dead before her. He had watched over her all of her life. He was a bridge and buffer between her and her father. Her heart felt like it would burst, it hurt so. Tears would not come. Words or cries would not come, and she could neither hear the subdued speech nor note the silent movements of the rest of the party.

Callista sat immobile on the other side of the still form. She shed no tears and uttered no sound. Her only movement was her hand that patted and gently stroked Scipio's shoulder.

Finally, the party had worked around Cynthia and Callista and Scipio's still form until they had prepared everything for the crossing. Owen Davis hobbled to her side and knelt. "Miss Montgomery! Miss Montgomery! Let me help you to the wagon. We will care for Scipio."

As she stood, the tears finally came in a flood. Deep wracking sobs welled up from the depths of her being. Bobby and Lon helped to lift her onto the wagon bed and gently laid her down on her bed.

Tom found a sunny clearing close by, and they took turns digging to finish the grave as quickly as possible. When they were done, they wrapped the body in a blanket and carried it to the graveside while Callista walked beside the body. Davis went back to the wagon and told Cynthia that they were ready and helped her to the graveside. He said a few prayers that he thought were appropriate from the many such hasty burials he had seen in the war. Cynthia was unable to speak, so they laid him in his final home and covered up the body. A cross was driven into the ground as a marker, and they moved back to the wagon.

All except Callista. She sat down by the grave and refused to move. No sweet word of comfort would make her leave. Finally, Callista looked up at Cynthia with tears streaming from her eyes. "He was mine. I love him. I cannot go away and leave him all alone. You bought my freedom. It is a precious gift, and I am grateful for it more than you can understand. Freedom means that I can decide what happens to me and where I go or where I stay. When I was little, my master told me a story about Callista; he said she was a girl that lived in the forest like my people did. Some bad god or something put a spell on her 'cause he wanted to control her, but a good goddess changed her into a bear. Then, to keep her from being hunted and killed, she put her in heaven as a star. God will take care of me here beside my man until He puts us both together in the heavens as stars." She sobbed and held Cynthia's hand so very tightly. "Don't you see that the story has come true? You are the good goddess. You protected me and set me free, and now I am a bear to live here in the woods waiting to go to heaven. I love you. Thank you."

The two women embraced for a long time, then kissed and parted.

Tom spoke softly and broke the gloom. "Folks, we got to do this tonight or we may never make it across. What do you want us to do with this wagon, Major?"

Owen Davis sat up. "Listen closely; we have to do this right or we may lose the wagon. We want to lay out the canvas. We will roll the wagon onto it and first sling the swivel gun under it to lower the center of gravity to help keep the floating wagon upright. Then we force the bundles of brush under the wagon to fill the space completely with something firm enough to give the canvas help in resisting the water pressure when the wagon is floating, but light enough to not drag it under. Without that support, the canvas will tear and fill, sinking the wagon. When it is stuffed as tight as we can make it, we wrap the package tightly with the canvas and tie it off with the ropes. We will pull it from the sand into the water with the mules until it floats or it doesn't float. If it doesn't float, we can drag it back to shore and try something else. If it does float, we use the boats that Tom's friends are bringing to tow the wagon and the horses and mules swimming to the other side. If we should run into a navy patrol, do not run; shout for help and let me do the talking. You are all a party that I recruited to help me after the cavalry escort abandoned me. Let's go!"

Three hours later, it was full dark and the wagon was bobbing in the water with its top about a foot out of the water. The oarsmen began pulling the wagon and stock west across the river. The wagon towed well, but some of the mules were beginning to tire. The lines to these halters were shortened to give the animals some support from the boats. As they passed from the east bank to the middle of the stream, the current lessened after they crossed the main channel. A harsh voice shouting, "Halt!" cut off their sigh of relief! "Identify yourself, or we will fire."

Owen Davis answered, "Major Owen Davis, U.S. Army, and his party. We are struggling. We need your help. Who are you?"

"Boat from the gunboat USS *Mohican*. Do not show any weapons. We are coming to board you." A torch flared about thirty yards away, and a long boat stroked toward them. In the bow of the long boat stood two husky sailors manning a swivel gun similar to the one now slung below the wagon.

Davis waved from the boat, calling to the sailors, "We need help; is your ship close by?"

When the long boat came within a few yards, they sheared off and lay parallel to the boat towing the wagon.

An ensign looked over the party and asked, "What is the trouble, Major? You look all right to me."

"We are towing a wagon with my papers and supplies. It is too much for us because the stock is tiring. I am afraid we will lose them if we don't get some help."

"Why did you try to cross this way? The army has a crossing point just a few miles north of here."

"We have been dodging Rebel cavalry for four days, and it has been two weeks since I left our lines on my mission. I had no firm idea of where we were, but I sure knew the Rebels were between us and where our army was north of the town."

The ensign said something to a man in the stern of the long boat. He rose and lit two torches and began to wave them in a pattern like semaphore. Then the ensign ordered the long boat on a circuit of the boat, animals, and wagons. When he completed his circuit, he told Major Davis that the gunboat would be along soon.

The noise of the gunboat's paddle wheels could be heard approaching, and the light from a number of torches on its decks made a fiery path across the water. It pulled alongside and, in a flurry of shouts and the patter of running feet, a whip was rigged and the first mule was lifted from the water. The others followed quickly, and the wagon was warped back to a heavier boom to be rigged for lifting out of the water.

While this flurry of activity was going on, Tom and his friends drifted silently away in their boat. From the first contact with the navy patrol, they had remained at the edge of the circle of light, silently watching. When it was plain that the party was relatively safe under the control of the Union navy, they simply let the current take them downstream safely out of sight.

On the deck of the steamer, Owen Davis collapsed in a spasm

of coughing and retching. When he was lifted to his feet by Bobby and Lon, the side of his face was red with blood. A naval officer showed them to a tiny bunk in the deckhouse and the limp form was stretched out and covered with a blanket. The young officer found Cynthia in the wardroom. He explained Major Davis's condition to her and told her that they would pull into the army base in a short time, and he could be transferred to a hospital.

Cynthia listened patiently. When he was through and looked quizzically at her, she only nodded and said, "He will not want that. He will not want to go to a hospital. He really does not need one. He's dying, you see." It was a matter of fact statement said quietly. She shook her head sadly, "He is a very brave man." She fell silent. When he offered her some coffee, she only nodded absently. He placed the mug before her and silently withdrew his questions unanswered.

At first light, the steamer came alongside a wharf projecting well into the river from a low, muddy bank. The river steamer-gunboat was moored, and they unloaded its cargo of mules, wagon, and people. As soon as all were ashore, including the major, who was supported again by Bobby and Lon, the boat sounded her whistle and began to pull away.

The major said, "We have to work fast and get the wagon unwrapped and the swivel and supplies reloaded before the dock workers come along and take too much interest. I can't help much. It is all on you. I am going to walk to the land end of the wharf and keep them busy. Come and get me when you have the things in the wagon. I will come back then for hitching up the mules. We have to find the headquarters."

Chapter 8

An hour later, the team was pulling the wagon up the muddy bank. The major put on his blouse and sidearms and sat on the wagon box with Cynthia. Bobby and Lon rode behind on their saddle mules. The wealth and plenty of the camp, as well as the smells of food, men, and smoke, mixed with the smell of animals, overwhelmed the habitually hungry Confederate soldiers. "My Lord, Bobby, how we going to win against all of this?"

"I don't know. I don't know," he answered gloomily.

Owen Davis climbed down from the wagon and entered a large tent with two sentinels. He was gone for over an hour as the little party waited nervously in a sea of Union blue. Cynthia retreated into the wagon and sat quietly in the heat of the stuffy shadows. Fear of discovery flickered in her heart as a flame, yet she shivered in the early July heat. She got out the Confederate safe conducts and the big colt pistol. She hid them in her clothes and slung the big pistol inside her skirts as she had learned to do when she was imprisoned in Kentucky. She felt desperately alone. Bobby and Lon sat subdued on the tailgate, saying little to each other.

When Owen Davis at last came out of the tent, he was white and sweating profusely. He staggered as he got to the wagon and almost fell against the wheel. The coughing started. His body was wracked with the spasms. Cynthia rushed to the wagon box from her hideaway. Bobby and Lon came from behind the wagon and took Major Davis by the arms and eased him down to a sitting position. He was bleeding again, and his face was wiped gently with a cloth. When the spasm was over, they lifted him to his feet and helped him into the wagon, where they stretched him out on his pallet.

He caught his breath and motioned for them to come close. "I told them that I had to continue my mission west of the river. We argued about it for a long time. I had to point out that there were large bodies of Confederates west of the river that would surely try to relieve Vicksburg by attacking our camp here or cutting our line of supply to the north or south. I was told that the cavalry could handle the mission, along with the navy. General Grant is not here. The chief of his staff wants me to write my report first and see a doctor next. I told him that I would write the report, but that I will submit my resignation as soon as it is finished. I told him that I had hired all of you to help me after you found me. He thinks Bobby is your brother and that you are along to do the cooking. We had better leave everything there, as it pleases them and is neat and logical. Cynthia, please stay out of sight as much as possible. The rest of us will not attract any attention, but your presence is unusual. My report should take only a day, tomorrow, to write. Then, we will leave headed north."

They all stared at him. "We have to head north at first. We will turn west as soon as we can safely do it. Meanwhile, I will try to get copies of the best maps available of the country to the westward without attracting too much attention."

The morning of the next day, they repacked the wagon with supplies drawn from the quartermaster. Owen Davis was able to get new boots and shoes for Bobby and Lon, as well as replenish the food, ammunition, blankets, socks, and underwear. Both men drew the line at blue coats, although the good woolen britches were acceptable to them because so many of them had been worn by other Confederates when their own wore out.

As the wagon moved toward the northern edge of the camp, a roar and a cheer rippled across the tent city. As the noise approached and passed them, Davis leaned down and asked a young lieutenant what the cheering was all about. "Vicksburg has surrendered unconditionally!" he shouted.

At the Union outpost line, Owen Davis spent a long time talking to the infantry and cavalry company commanders about what lay to the west and north. He discovered that the Rebel forces opposing them were scattered and not well disciplined. General Dick Taylor was far to the south near Donaldsonville. The roads as far west as they had ridden were quiet, but there were many reports of banditry along the road. They were waved through with a good luck wish.

About a half mile farther west, they found the Confederate outpost concealed at the edge of a small copse by the roadside. The picket chatted easily with Bobby and Lon and simply waved the wagon through. He asked them if their visit to the Yankee camp had been profitable. They simply grunted agreement and rode on ahead of the wagon. As the wagon passed, the soldiers called out a warning to beware of jayhawkers along the road.

By first light, they had moved some ten miles deep into Confederate territory. They picked a campsite off the road with a concealing screen between them and the road. They rested during the day and moved onto the road at dark. Bobby and Lon rode ahead on mules while Cynthia brought the wagon slowly along behind. Owen Davis, still exhausted by the labor of the last week, lay in full uniform in the bed of the wagon.

In the following week, they covered sixty miles, but Owen Davis was weakening badly. His coughing and rasping breath told the story of his coming death in eloquent terms. Although his exhausted frame craved sleep and rest, he could not be comfortable lying down. Rolled blankets propped him up to keep him from simply tumbling over as the wagon lurched and bumped. His coughing brought up bloody foam whose red and white colors matched the pallor of his skin and the brilliant red spots that colored each cheek. When it was near the end, they stopped in a wood and spent the day trying to ease his suffering. About noon, he lost consciousness. By early afternoon, he was gone, his wasted body shrunken and limp from his last fight.

They washed his body and dressed him in his uniform. They laid him to rest and marked his grave with a sturdy cross that they made of rough-cut oak branches. At dawn, they rolled west toward Shreveport.

A few conversations with farmers along the road warned them

again about jayhawkers and stragglers. There was little they could do other than have one person ride ahead scouting for trouble as the other followed the wagon as rear guard. Their weakness in numbers haunted them. They had now half the fighting strength that they'd had on the other side of the Mississippi. They cleaned and checked their weapons every night before dark. The swivel gun could be cocked and fired instantly.

Heat became their constant companion, and flies and all manner of insects were their escorts. They fashioned hoods to protect the heads and ears of the mules. Fatigue eroded their energy and alertness, but there was no rest.

Fire of several rifles from the brush on the right of the road swept Bobby from his saddle. Cynthia reined the mules left across the road to give the swivel gun a clear field of fire from the right front of the wagon. Lon spurred forward at a gallop closing to the left, partially protected from being overrun by the attackers. Cynthia set the brake and rolled backward from the wagon seat to cock and point the still-covered swivel gun.

The jayhawkers rushed down the road at the wagon , ignoring Bobby's fallen form. Their shouts and yells of triumph turned Cynthia's blood cold and made her palms wet with sweat as she grasped the lanyard of the gun with her right hand and pointed the still-concealed gun with her left. She dimly heard Lon's Rebel yell as he thundered forward. The first jayhawker was only ten yards away when Cynthia fired the swivel gun. Thunder, flame, and a hail of pistol balls raked the loose column of shouting men. Men and horses screamed and fell as the lead balls tore through clothing, equipment, men, and animals.

Lon dismounted in a cloud of dust as his mount squatted down to keep from plunging into the harnessed mules pulling the wagon. Lon leveled his rifle and shot one of the few remaining mounted jayhawkers. He reloaded while Cynthia snatched up a rifle from the rack in the wagon and shot at another. The jayhawkers turned tail and ran, but Lon was able to shoot another one before he could get out of range. He vaulted the wagon tongue and, fixing his bayonet, trotted up the road, finishing off the living outlaws. When he had dispatched the last one, he ran on to Bobby's inert body.

He lifted Bobby's head gently and spoke to him, tenderly calling his name again and again. Kneeling, he lifted the limp form to his breast and cradled him in his arms as a sleeping child. Lon slowly rocked back and forth, crooning to his friend.

Cynthia caught Bobby's mule and tied its reins to the tailgate of the wagon and drove forward through the carnage to stop beside the two friends. She climbed down and knelt beside them. For a long time she said nothing. Finally, she rose and got a cloth from the wagon. She wet it and gently washed Bobby's face. Lon walked over and picked up Bobby's hat. He dusted it off and put it on the dead man's breast. "He was right proud of that hat. He said it made him look jaunty."

"He was right. It did," she said.

They wrapped him in his blanket and buried him south of the road in the corner of a meadow.

That night she heard Lon weeping softly and calling Bobby's name.

Two days later, they ran into a patrol from Colonel Tom Green's Texas cavalry. The patrol took them back to Colonel Green. The old Indian fighter fixed them with his dark, deep-set eyes. "Tell me who you are and where you come from."

Cynthia produced the pass from Bedford Forrest and remained silent. Green read the pass carefully and then looked searchingly at her for a long time in silence. For a full three minutes, they sat silently assessing each other. "Tell me," he commanded. She quietly told him the whole story. He listened carefully

"I think it best that you go directly to see General Taylor in Shreveport. I have some men who need to go back to the hospital there. According to what you have told me, they should be in good hands traveling with you. They will also provide you with some protection that is sorely needed along that road. Can you make room for them in your wagon?"

"How many do you have, Colonel, and what condition are they in?"

Cynthia and Lon left the next morning with six of Colonel Green's Texans in the wagon and two on their own mounts.

Chapter 9

At the hospital at Shreveport, Cynthia was given directions to Mr. Luave's house where General Taylor was staying. At the house she was received reluctantly until she presented Bedford Forrest's pass and a letter from Colonel Tom Green. She was told that the general was very busy, but the general's aide would give him word about her as soon as they could break into his deliberations.

As she waited, two little girls peeked into the room. She smiled and they came to her. "Who are you?" they asked.

"I am Cynthia. Tell me your names."

"I am Betty and this is Louise. Our Papa is General Taylor. Are you here to talk to Papa?"

"Yes, but I would like to talk to you until I see him."

The girls chatted happily for a few minutes until a voice called their names. A slender, dark-haired, very pretty woman only a few years older than Cynthia came into the room. "I do hope they have not bothered you," she said to Cynthia.

"Oh, no. They are charming and quite well behaved. You must be Mrs. Taylor. Pardon me for being so presumptuous, but I am Cynthia Montgomery. My father served under General Taylor's father in the Mexican War."

" And you bring a message from him to the general?" she asked.

All of the strain of the journey suddenly descended onto her shoulders with this innocent question. Cynthia had before her the stark fact that she did not even know if her father was alive. The man she loved was lost in the mists of war and might be dead, too. All of the men that she had known and respected were dead except Lon. She had seen the aftermath of the battle and held the hands of dying boys only a few years younger than she, and had answered their heartbreaking cries as a mother. She had seen the horror of battlefields firsthand—seen and smelled the fresh gore and bitter smoke of burned powder. She had managed the destruction of men and horses at ranges so short that she could see the color of their eyes. Despair flooded her soul and crushed her spirit. She sat and she wept. Her sobs shook her body and robbed her of all control.

Mrs. Taylor spoke softly and put an arm around her shoulders. After a moment, she gently lifted Cynthia and walked her back into the house.

Late in the afternoon, Cynthia woke from exhausted sleep. It took a while for her to puzzle out where she was and why her heart still felt like stone. Sadness weighed her down, but her tears were all used up. The ache and longing for her father and John were physical pain. She did not know if they were gone, but she felt as though she must mourn for them now. Alone. Alone. Empty.

Mimi Taylor came in and sat down beside her. "We have something for you to eat, and hot water is coming for you to wash in. My maid will be here to assist you. We have unloaded your wagon. Your things have been brought into the house, and my maid has taken things to the laundress. Your soldier has been quartered with the general's guards."

"Oh! I was so overcome, I forgot about poor Lon. You cannot know what we have been through."

Mimi gave Cynthia an appraising look and said, "I know more about grief than you might think."

Cynthia flushed scarlet. "I am sorry. I know you only by your kindness. I do not know your burdens, but I do know that southern women have all known great pain and heartache. I was giving in to my own sorrow."

"I lost my two baby boys to scarlet fever a short time ago. My heart is breaking. My little Zack died in a day and a half. My sweet little Dixie lingered for three weeks. Nothing, scarcely anything, was left of him. It was enough to soften the hardest heart to witness the sufferings that my sweet little man went through during the last twenty-four hours of his short, happy life. Only Louise and Betsy survived," Mimi said with downcast eyes.

Later that week Cynthia was called in to see General Taylor. The handsome man with the grace and manners of a courtier received her graciously. He listened to her story and read her passes, including the one from Owen Davis. He was quiet when she finished with her intention to go on to Texas as soon as possible.

After a time he spoke. "Miss Montgomery, I know and respect your father as did my father before me. To honor him, I will do anything for you in my power. I must tell you that the journey before you is a long and dangerous one. It is neither safe nor fitting that you should travel that road protected only by your one escort. Surely, your journey and its dangers to this point have made that plain to you. You began with three escorts and now have only one. Despite the unusual nature of your defenses, you have been incredibly lucky so far. In addition, it is not suitable for a young lady of your station to travel unaccompanied by other females.

"Mrs. Taylor has asked that you rest here from your journey for a while until companions and an escort of adequate strength can be assembled to see you safely to your destination. Were I not to assure your safety and protection in that way, I would not serve your father or you as my honor and duty direct."

"General, I will do as you ask and will be honored to be a guest in your home for a time. I would ask, if you can do so, that you find out about my father and Lieutenant John K. McKenzie of the Seventh Kentucky Cavalry in General John Hunt Morgan's command."

The weeks passed slowly, although Mimi and her two beautiful daughters became her constant companions in play and in the tasks of organizing a large and active household. After a month, General Taylor asked her into his office and told her the sad news of her father's death of pneumonia. He assured her that her father had been well cared for by his servants and the people of his district. The local Union army commander had known Homer Montgomery during the Mexican War. He attended the funeral and saw that proper honors were accorded a gallant and good man. The burial party included some sergeants from the Old Mexican War Army, who participated in the rendering of honors. No man could have been accorded more respect and humanity. "May God, give him rest!

"I have written to Richmond and to General Bragg with the Army of Tennessee, trying to find some word of Lieutenant McKenzie. They have no word of him thus far. His name has not appeared on the lists of prisoners taken after the destruction of General Morgan's command in the fight at Buffington Island, Ohio, or on the lists of those killed in that fight printed in the northern newspapers. We hold out the hope that he escaped capture and is working his way back to our lines. I regret that I can tell you nothing more."

In the fall, when the roads were dry and the weather began to cool, Cynthia was introduced to her companions for the onward trip to Texas. Mrs. Bennett was a tall, slender woman of uncertain age with a fine, strong face and a character to match. She had come to the army with her husband, who served as a sergeant in Tom Green's cavalry. He had survived a chest wound and lost an eye in fights against the Union troopers. He was to command her escort. Serene, the other female companion, was a small woman. Quiet. Her face was expressionless most of the time. She had a reputation as a good cook and reliable worker. She volunteered to go along, but told no one why she wanted to go. The rest of the escort was made up of a dozen men with disabling injuries that prevented them from a return to active service. Each of them could handle a musket and was all too familiar with the stress of combat. Counting Lon and Cynthia, there were fourteen men and three women in the party.

They were allocated a wagon and a team of mules to carry the supplies, arms, and equipment of the escort. Lon spat contemptuously when he saw the wagon, harness, and mules.

"Miss Cynthia, that thing won't make it across the Sabine River, let alone all the way to Plano."

"But, we need it, Lon. Our own wagon is not big enough to haul all of their equipment as well as our own."

"Can you get me a week before we go, miss? I know where I can find some tools. If I can find some decent lumber instead of the green trash they use here, I will strengthen it all I can. I'm going to talk to Sergeant Bennett to get him to help me out."

"All right, Lon. I will ask the general if we can wait a few days. I am sure he will not mind."

By sundown, Lon had moved the wagon away from the head-quarters to a back yard where it was away from the notice of the many officers coming and going at the headquarters of General Taylor. Every so often, the men of the escort would be seen walking into that yard carrying a board, some tool, or once, even a keg of nails. Some of the artillery units noticed small bits of harness missing. The quartermaster found himself short of paint, but it was all small losses, so nobody complained too much.

On Wednesday, two days before their departure, Lon took their wagon down to the same yard to do some repairs. When Cynthia walked down to see how things were coming along, Sergeant Bennett intercepted her and took her to the store house where the supplies were stacked and kept her busy all afternoon checking and rechecking the supplies. He had two men of the escort stack the stores in a separate pile for each wagon. Each pile was arranged from front to back to load stores in the reverse order of when they would be needed. The sergeant emphasized that he wanted to be on the march at first light—before, if possible.

Cynthia agreed, and he escorted her back to say her farewells to the general and Mrs. Taylor. They entertained her at dinner and wished her good night with many sad looks. Most difficult of all was saying goodbye to the two little girls.

Chapter 10

As the darkness made its barely perceptible change from opaque blackness to the beginning of day, Cynthia heard the clink of harness and rumble of wagon wheels outside. She finished dressing and went down the stairs to snatch a bite of breakfast. The house servants brought down her bundles and chests. While she ate, her things were loaded into the wagon under Sergeant Bennett's eagle eye.

Mimi came in with the general and joined her for a light meal. Mimi sat morosely watching Cynthia and picking at her own plate. Finally the tears came. "I shall miss you so, my dear. The girls will have no playmate, and I will have no companion with whom I can whisper and laugh. There is so little to laugh about without you."

Cynthia rose and came around the table to her friend's side. She circled her with her arms and held her close. "Mimi, you know that I love you. You know, too, that I must go if there is any chance of finding my John. He does not know where else I might be, other than where he told me he would come to me. I do not know if he lives or has been killed. Even the general has not been able to get word of him after months of trying. I promise to write to you and to come back to you someday, if God grants me that gift."

General Taylor stood beside her and, taking her hand, he raised her to her feet. Mimi rose and stood beside him.

"Miss Montgomery, you are a part of our lives and a valued member of our family. It is painful to all of us to surrender you to your quest. You must remember that you are always welcome and can call upon me for anything that is in my power to give." He bent to kiss her hand, then he turned and walked to the door. "I must see that your party is ready to start. Come along as soon as you have finished your goodbyes."

He strode out the door and, after a few moments of silence, they heard his fine voice laughing uproariously. Holding hands, Mimi and Cynthia hurried out to see what the merriment was all about. "It is the first time that I have heard him laugh…in months," she finished lamely.

When they got to the front door, they found Sergeant Bennett standing before the escort that was formed in two ranks in new uniforms with polished arms and equipment. But there was more. The two wagons were freshly painted in a bright green with red trim, the harness was cleaned, and the black iron and brass was polished. Snowy new canvas covered both wagons marked with the military "CS." Most noticeable were the mules. In addition to the original Montgomery mule that Scipio had brought, there were three more big strapping animals with Confederate brands that undoubtedly belonged to some Confederate artillery unit until last night.

Sergeant Bennett called, "Escort, attention! General, the escort is ready for duty."

"Thank you, Sergeant Bennett. I will inspect the men. Miss Montgomery, will you do me the honor of accompanying me on my inspection and receiving the salute?"

"Thank you, General. I am honored to accept."

They walked through the ranks slowly, looking carefully at each man. After they had completed the circuit and returned to the front of the formation, General Taylor spoke quietly to Sergeant Bennett. "It seems that I have picked the best possible man to carry out this important task. I am wondering if I should have kept you and made you my quartermaster general." Then louder, "The men look well, Sergeant. I will expect them to perform in an outstanding manner until their task is complete. You will be under the orders of Miss Montgomery until she releases you. She will hold the rank of lieutenant on my staff and all the authority that rank confers.

"Miss Montgomery, the escort is under your orders."

The march west was a smooth, almost pleasant progress. Sergeant Bennett controlled the escort with the sure hand of an experienced professional. A point and rear guard was always out. Sentinels were posted at rests and all night every night. The men were kept clean and alert. Arms were always clean and ready.

At nights, the two wagons were parked tongue across tongue pointing toward the road. The swivel gun was always re-primed and pointed toward the road. One of the two sentinels on duty was always on the gun. The other sentinel walked in a "u" shaped pattern around the open end of the "v" where the mules were picketed.

Serene cooked for the party in the morning and in the evening. The noon meal was usually some bread and dried beef or something left from breakfast. Mrs. Bennett oversaw the preparation and clean up, and slept with her husband under Cynthia's wagon. Serene slept in the other wagon. Fires were out before sunset and not lighted in the morning until Sergeant Bennett and two men made a long patrol all around the camp. By the end of the first week on the road, the orderly routine of the camp and road was a smoothly functioning habit with all of the party.

On the eighth day, one of the escort soldiers complained of a bad headache and stomach pain. Mrs. Bennett put him on a pallet on the tailgate of the second wagon. By the noon halt he was weak and very feverish. They gave him water for his thirst, but he often vomited it up. The pains in his gut made him moan, and by late afternoon his fever had stepped up to the point where his skin felt as if it were on fire. Sergeant Bennett opened his clothes to look at the scar on his chest wound to see if infection was the problem. He found no specific tenderness on the wound but general sensitivity and a welter of rose-colored spots on the man's chest and stomach. He gloomily closed the shirt over the chest and shook his head.

"Miss Cynthia, may I speak to you in private?"

"Yes, of course. Let's walk along the road. Ask Mrs. Bennett to come along. I expect she will need to know what we are talking about."

A moment later, Mrs. Bennett and the sergeant walked west along the ruts of the road to Dallas with Cynthia.

"What do you want to tell me?" Cynthia asked.

"I'm pretty sure the boy has typhoid. He is dying."

"How do you know? Are you sure?"

"I haven't seen it since 1861, but I remember it pretty well. Yes, miss. I am sure. He will probably die in the morning if he doesn't die tonight."

"Is there nothing we can do?"

"No, miss. There's not a thing that we can do for him. For the rest of us, we need to stay away from him. I've seen this sweep through a company and kill three quarters of the men."

"What shall we do?"

"Well, miss, we probably ought to bury him as soon as he dies and then move on until we find a good source of water, some shelter, and level ground. When we find that, we should camp and stay there 'til the disease has burned itself out."

The boy died that night before midnight. Two men were set to digging his grave and burying him. Mrs. Bennett saw to it that they washed thoroughly with lye soap and put on new clothes. Their clothes, along with the dead boy's clothes, were burned.

Within half an hour, Sergeant Bennett had them on the march again. No one complained too much. Every veteran in the escort had seen typhoid from close up or far away, and they were genuinely frightened of it.

They marched through breakfast and did not find a decent campsite until nearly noon. At supper, four of the men refused anything to eat, saying they were not hungry. By moonrise they were complaining of the same symptoms shown by the first boy. One of them lasted three days. On the fifth day, Cynthia went to bed with fever and stomach cramps.

In the middle of the night, she awakened to a disturbing sound. She did not feel as bad as she thought she would, but she certainly did not feel well. She finally identified the sound as Serene's sobs.

"Serene! Is that you?"

"Yes, miss."

"Come here, I need you."

Serene's face was haggard and streaked with tears.

"Where is Mrs. Bennett?"

"She's asleep, miss."

"Why are you crying, Serene?"

"'Cause I'm bad luck for everybody who is kind to me. Everywhere that I go and stay, people get sick and die. Do they die like this everywhere, miss? I'm so afraid. I came with you to run away. I can't stand it anymore."

Cynthia thought for a long time before she spoke. Her mind raced over the many conversations between the doctors in the hospital in Chattanooga. They talked about a Doctor Oliver Wendell Holmes and his ideas about how sickness was spread. One of the doctors had talked a long time about typhoid. He believed it might spread from one man to another, but he did not know how it was passed. The association of this plain girl with such a terrible man killer was absurd, but Serene said that everywhere she went, people got the disease.

"Have you ever been sick like this, Serene?"

"Oh, no miss! I had my head hurt and my belly too, but I didn't die," she sobbed.

"All right, Serene, go to bed. We will decide what to do in the morning."

Cynthia thought for a while and then went to wake up Mrs. Bennett. The older woman was awake instantly. Her husband stirred beside her and came up with a Remington army revolver in his hand.

"What is it, miss?" He spoke very softly without any exhalation of air so that his words carried in the still night no farther than to Cynthia's ears.

"I need to talk to you both. The danger is here, but we cannot fight it with our usual weapons."

"Miss?"

"I am sorry; I did not intend to talk in riddles. I am very worried. Some doctors whom I helped last year believed that this typhoid is passed from person to person. They do not know how. Serene just told me a few minutes ago that everywhere she goes, the disease appears. I am worried that if the doctors are correct, then Serene may have brought the disease to us. I do not know if this is true. I also think that I may have it. You do not seem to have it, and I do not know why, if most of the rest of us do. Lon does not have it, but he told me that he had it early in the war and survived."

The Bennetts were silent. Then she explained, "I have cooked separately for my husband because he wanted to eat first so that he could set the guards and go with the morning patrols. I ate with him. In every other respect, there has been no difference between our contact with Serene and her contact with everyone but you. I have prepared your meals at the same time as I cooked for my husband so that you could do your packing or unpacking without delaying our camp at night or our departure in the morning. Yesterday, you took a cup of coffee from her."

Cynthia's heart sank as though a judge had pronounced a death sentence on her. She did not feel well, but the disease had not followed the rapid destruction of her health that had happened in all of the other cases.

The quaver in her voice gave away her fear when she said, "What shall we do?"

Mrs. Bennett's voice softened as she answered, "We must stop Serene from handling any food or drink. You must go to your bunk and stay there. Only my husband and I will cook for you or serve you anything. Lon will have to be our sentinel when every other person is sick. From what my husband tells me, the rest will probably get sick today or tonight. If they are going to live, we will know in a few days. I do not know how long it will take for them to recover. Perhaps Lon can tell us.

"Go to bed now, miss. Tom and I will take care of the camp until you are feeling better."

In the morning, Cynthia did not feel better. She was hot to the touch and experiencing stomach pain that was quite severe. Mrs. Bennett kept her in bed and looked to the camp. The guards coming off the early watch were not hungry and complained of the same symptoms first shown by the boy a few days before. Some of them were frightened by the implications of that unwelcome news, but they were too miserable to do anything but lie down. Mrs. Bennett woke up Serene and told her to not cook, as no one was hungry. She appointed her the caretaker of the sick men. Mrs. Bennett strictly enforced the requirement that Serene wash her hands after handling anything belonging to the sick men.

By the next morning, every man in camp but Sergeant Bennett and Lon was prostrate on his blankets, and by noon the deaths began. The men, weakened by their wounds and the march, simply could not fight off the destructive power of the infection. Only Cynthia fought on. Mrs. Bennett made her drink water and beef broth, and kept her body and bedding clean. In response to a questioning look from her husband, she only shrugged and shook her head.

Lon was able to scratch out a long, shallow trench for a mass grave, and each man who died was buried as soon as he expired. "Hadn't we ought to get away from here, Tom?" he asked.

"I don't much like it either, but we want to give Miss Montgomery as good a chance as we can give her."

"I sure feel like that too. I've known her ever since she came to the hospital in Chattanooga more than a year ago. You've never seen anything like it. She was everywhere. She was every man's sister and mother and nurse. I've watched her hold the hand of a dying man all day and into the night and then heard her cry in her room 'til morning. The next day she was doing it again. I'd do anything for her, and so would all of us who were in that hospital—but they ain't here now. Is there anything your wife wants done that I can do?"

"I don't think so, Lon, but I'll ask her."

"How come Serene ain't cooking anymore? Looks like to me your wife's got too much on her now to take that on too."

The big man was silent with his remaining eye shut. Lon was not sure that he had heard him.

"Lon, we think it best that Serene not cook until we find out where this thing came from. I was in the hospital with all of these men. None of them was anywhere near typhoid for a long time before we started. You and Miss Montgomery weren't either, as you well know. The only one of all of us of whom we know very little is Serene. There are a lot of tasks to be done around camp that she can do."

"I'll try to keep an eye on her. She seems like a good person. I am sure she wouldn't hurt anybody on purpose. Last night I saw her wandering around. As we get farther north, it begins to get more dangerous. You know about Comanches, Tom."

"Yes, I sure do. Come to that, it's time to start watching for signs. You and I can change off riding a big circle around the camp a couple of times a day. Tell Serene to stay close by, and tell her why."

"Sounds good! I'll do it."

Chapter 11

Tom Bennett found what he was worried about the next afternoon. It was a feather with paint on it and the track of a single pony shod with rawhide. "Damn! Damn! Damn! Why now?"

When he got back to camp, he had a quiet conversation with Lon and his wife. "Lon, tell Serene, and tell her why she should stay close to camp. Recheck the charges in all of the rifles and keep them handy. On our rides, we go fully armed."

Serene listened to Lon carefully. "I know what to do. Don't worry about me, Lon. I been thinking about things that I can do to help out. I just thought of another one."

The night passed slowly. The three healthy members of the caravan took turns awake and asleep so that each got about four hours of sleep while the others kept watch. Tom Bennett took the cover off of Cynthia's wagon so the swivel gun could fire in any direction. One watcher sat at the gun with the two wagons, tongues crossed and the wagon bodies forming a "V."

The animals were picketed close in at the open end of the "V." Tom had also cut posts and strung rope fences to slow a rush into the open end of the "V." The guard at that end sat behind boxes for protection from a shot in the darkness. Several small fires were lit well away from the wagons to illuminate the ground outside of that end of the camp.

There was a good bit of stirring about in the brush well outside of the camp, but no attempt was made during darkness. Tom made everyone stay put until well after sunup. Mrs. Bennett brought each person some food to eat at his post and refilled the canteens from the water barrel. She took care of watering the mules and giving them some fodder. About mid morning, they changed positions. Lon moved to the swivel and Tom did camp chores while Serene sat at the open end of the "V." Mrs. Bennett saw to Cynthia and reported her sleeping deeply and quietly. The fever seemed to have abated. Serene heard the news with elation. She turned and stood up to clap her hands.

The five Comanches came out of the brush in a deadly silent rush toward Serene's position. "Tom! Indians!" Mrs. Bennett's scream was too late. Serene and the mules blocked the swivel field of fire, and Serene stood, turned, and froze at the sight of the glaring eyes and bronze faces that were upon her. The leading Indian crashed his horse into the rope fence and took it down, but he tumbled head over heels into the camp. As he struggled out from under the hooves of the mules, Mrs. Bennett split his head open with the fire shovel. Lon and Tom used their pistols, but the second Indian had already snatched Serene by the hair and dragged her, screaming, back toward the brush. The Indians fired at Lon and Tom but missed. They reined their horses around and galloped back to the brush in a hail of fire.

The three could hear Serene's screams only for a few seconds after they lost sight of the Indians in the brush. They feared the worst, but Tom grabbed Lon by the arm and kept him from following.

"Let me go, Tom! I got to try to save her."

"It's too late, Lon. There are at least four of them out there and maybe one or two more to cover their back trail. You will be plain to see as you head for that brush, and they will down you before you get to the brush; then they will wait for me to come get you."

"What if I circle around from the far side of the camp?"

"You still got to fight four of them, and you don't know that they will be nice and all in one place waiting for you. Look here, Lon. Mrs. Bennett and I noticed that you felt special about Serene. We understand what you are feeling now. You can't go get yourself killed without having a chance to get her back. Sometimes if an Indian captive survives the first few days, they can be ransomed or rescued. When we find out exactly where she winds up, we can get some men and go get her.

"Now, we got to stay awake through the night till morning to be sure they don't come back."

Two miles west of the wagon camp, the Indians dumped Serene unceremoniously on the ground and turned to one of their number who was bleeding from a shoulder wound. Serene watched for a moment and then got a water-skin from one of the Indian saddles and brought it to the men. They looked at her blankly, but took it and went back to caring for the wounded man. Serene rummaged in more saddlebags, and, after starting a very small fire, she began to cook for them.

Book Three

Smiting The
Enemy—
The Old Man's
Dream

Chapter 1

The gray column had headed north for days now. There had been feints to the east and west, but the general course was a thrust toward the Ohio River. Small Union garrisons in its way were gobbled up with ease and paroled. Each of Morgan's well-established deceptions was practiced to keep the blue armies guessing as to his object and his present location.

General Hurlburt was studying the big map when Captain Michaelman entered his tent.

"Any news about Morgan, Jimmy?"

"Too much, General. I have messages here that assure me that Morgan is bound for Lexington again, Louisville, and Bardstown. His scouts have been reported outside all of these places. Citizens and officers send to tell us that they overheard his officers talking about being in each of these places by tonight or tomorrow.

"The fact of the matter is that he could be at any of them, and he probably has sent some of his men to each of them. As to overhearing conversations between Morgan's officers about where they will be tonight or tomorrow, we have been fooled by that one before."

"Don't remind me, Jimmy. The old fox has kept us at bay this way for a long time. It may be that what we need to do is try to divine what he wants to do rather than where he wants to go. What do you think he's trying to do?"

Captain Michaelman stood beside the older man for several minutes, studying the map and shuffling through his messages. "He is going north, sir."

Hurlburt was exasperated. "Goddamit! I know that. Which city is he after?"

"No, no, General. I mean that he is going to the North. The place, not the direction."

"Ah! What makes you think that?"

"He has never held a town before. He has only cavalry with him, as usual. He needs infantry and guns to hold a city. So if he has none of those resources, what good is a city to him?"

"What good is going into the North to him?"

Michaelman thought hard for a while before answering. "Draw off troops from other successful operations that we are conducting. We know Lee's army is in Pennsylvania. We also have a Mississippi force surrounding Vicksburg. Any forces that Morgan can draw off will help those Confederates. He might also be thinking of the prison camps in Chicago, Alton, or Columbus. He could multiply his numbers by a factor of five at either one of those places. They may also want to raise the Copperheads."

"Well, that sounds reasonable. I am going to warn the general."

That afternoon Morgan's advance party lured two steamboats to shore and captured them. The following day the entire division crossed the Ohio River on the two boats and then burned them. Striking north first and then turning east, Morgan's seasoned troopers bluffed, battered, and by-passed local militia units. By using multiple routes from time to time, Morgan hid the location of the main body of his command from efforts to block his progress. Behind him was a more dangerous threat. General Hobson's Union cavalry brigade led by Wolford's 1st Kentucky Cavalry (Union) had crossed the Ohio with the help of civilian river traffic and was hot on the trail. Wolford had sparred with Morgan for the entire war and was determined to catch him and destroy his command. He had a force equal to Morgan's and was constantly being aided and reinforced by other Union commands.

The days to Cincinnati were hot and tiring, but Morgan's men had done as much and more before. Here, however, there was no place or time for rest for man or beast. They knew that the Union cavalry was close behind and that General Ambrose Burnside was in the city with thousands of troops and militia. The risk of major bodies of blue troops in and around Cincinnati was real. The lack of an extensive network of reliable information north of the Ohio River was telling on his ability to feint and maneuver. Support by the Copperheads was almost nonexistent. Although guides were captured at each successive town and threatened with death if they misled the Confederate column, the risk of some guide leading them astray or into a trap was a constant worry. When each successive guide had out-ridden his local knowledge, he was released after being allowed to hear a conference between Morgan and other officers about some false destination. "Lightning" Ellsworth, the telegrapher, spent every stationary moment up a telegraph pole, sending false messages to support the deception practiced on the former guides. On the eleventh of July, Morgan's men discovered the news of Gettysburg and Vicksburg. It was a blow that robbed them of certain assurance. Gloom descended on the gray raiders, and anger, too.

On the outskirts of Cincinnati, Morgan summoned men of his command who had lived in the city and knew the area well.

"Captain Taylor, reporting, General."

"I understand you lived for some time in Cincinnati?"

"Yes, General. I am quite familiar with it, as are two others whom I have brought with me."

"I want you to go into the city and find out how ready they are. If you can discover anything about their plans, it will be valuable to us. I can just give you a few hours. Will that be enough?"

"Yes, General, that will be enough. Shall we meet back here?"

"Yes, but I cannot wait for you if it takes more time. A strong force of cavalry is in pursuit behind us. If they get close, we will have to move on. Move eastward parallel to the river. I intend to pass the city to the north if I can, but I need to know if there is a force strong enough and energetic enough to block my way. Get me that information."

Jimmy Michaelman snapped his fingers and slapped his thigh. "I've got him!" He sat down at his field desk and began to write furiously. As soon as he finished, he shouted for an orderly. General Hurlburt came in at the same time as the enlisted man. "What's up, Jimmy? I heard you shout."

"Just a minute, General. Soldier, take these messages to the military telegraph office and tell them to get them on the wire right away. I want answers back as soon as they are received.

"Sorry, General. Every minute counts. I think I know for sure what Morgan is doing. I have sent messages to telegraph stations in a big arc around Morgan. They are to report any actual sighting giving the size and direction of movement. They are to report every half hour so that we know as much about where he isn't as we know about where he is. I am convinced that he is headed east along the Ohio River for a crossing back to the South. As soon as we can confirm that, we can get troops ahead of him and gun boats on the river to bag him."

Outside Cincinnati, a few hours later, late at night, Captain Taylor and his men returned to Morgan's column. "Ah! Captain Taylor. You made it just in time. What news did you bring us?"

"They are in disarray. There is a small part of the Yankee 9th Kentucky Cavalry camped in a park, and some veteran infantry, too. Much of the rest of what they have are untried troops or militia. They do not know where we are or what our intentions are, so they will defend the city from attack. They would be much more than we could handle in that role, but I doubt they will come out after us looking for a fight."

"As long as they stay in place for a day and a half, we will be past them. Tell the men to get ready to move," Morgan directed his staff officers.

The short rest was not enough when the command began moving again. Hours stretched out to dawn. The morning sun burned into their eyes, and the heat of the day cooked off the moisture from their bodies. Dust like talcum hung in the air. There were no halts for rest. By sundown the straggling had gotten very bad, and officers rode to the rear of their commands to keep men moving. Even darkness gave no concealment or healing rest. Legs and backs ached and burned. Constantly plodding along, the sad-dletree pounded the pelvis and cut off circulation to the legs. Legs without feeling could not lift the body away from the pressure. The pain was agonizing and unbearable. Animals already run down began to drop out of the column. Men who dismounted needed help to remount. Finally, after thirty-six hours, the head of the column found a field northeast of the city and stopped in the fresh grass. Men who could not lift a leg to dismount simply fell from their saddles and slept where they fell. Only a few were left to mount any guard and begin to water and care for the animals.

A few hours of sleep were only enough to get the men back on their feet to care for the stock and keep them moving. Each day followed the same pattern. Hard riding and short rests. Little vicious skirmishes with militia in front and army cavalry behind. Farm horses were switched for broken down cavalry horses, then broke down even faster. The constant pressure from behind and the certainty that the general direction of the movement of the column to the east would soon allow a significant Union force to get in front of them and bring them to bay haunted every man. They had to get to a river crossing before that happened, but the river was up and the fords were too deep.

A rattle of gunfire close behind them shook dozing troopers awake. Colonel Huffman shouted, "John, try to block the north road and keep them from getting ahead of us on that side. I'll try to send you some help!" John waved his arm in acknowledgment and shouted to the troop to follow him. They spurred across the large pasture toward the northwest corner. Half of the troop peeled off and lined the fence from the corner beside the east-west road southward back toward the main body. John urged his exhausted horse over the gate, but his troop's tired horses refused and jammed up at the gate onto the road. Two troopers dismounted to open the gate, but they were too late. The men along the fence opened fire on a thundering column of blue-coated cavalry hurtling down the road from the west. The blue soldiers returned fire from the saddle and closed on John alone blocking the road. He emptied a pistol at the leaders and put spurs to his mount. The right foreleg of the tough little horse hit the top bar of the gate leading to the field on the north side of the road and checked his momentum enough to unbalance him and retard his progress over the bars.

His horse fell, spilling John half out of the saddle. His head hit the gatepost a glancing blow. He was stunned but not unconscious.

The horse dragged himself back to his legs. He was quivering and shaken. John slid groggily out of the saddle and turned back toward the road. It was packed with blue men. Some were passing by, punching past John's small force without a pause. Others were struggling to get past the south side gate to John's men, firing almost point blank at them. John staggered toward the fight, drawing his other pistol. A big Yank looked over his shoulder and caught sight of the gray officer coming toward them from their rear.

"Look out, boys! They are behind us!" His cry brought a startled reaction from the men closest to John. The others seemed to not hear and kept up their fight to get at the Confederates in the pasture on the other side of the road. Two Yanks closest to John aimed their carbines at him and blazed away. Their shots cracked by him, but the muzzle blast burned his face and uniform. He thrust his second pistol at them and fired three times. He hit both of them and they tumbled backward. Suddenly the lane was empty. He could see the bodies of some of his men in the pasture opposite, bodies of blue cavalrymen in the lane, and he could hear the rush of more hooves shaking the ground as they came down the road at a full gallop.

Alone, he ran across the field pursued by whistling pistol balls. He scooped up his horse's reins and darted into a little copse at the far side of the field. The sound of firing filled the air as the terrible thunder of a summer storm. It rolled back and forth across the fields, spreading the fear and fire of war across the peaceful farms and woods of Ohio. The passage of troops along the road between him and Morgan's men was almost continuous.

After a long and anxious wait, he decided that he could not go straight back to the command. He would have to move to the north and east and catch up with them there or cross the Ohio and follow them south. He began to move carefully east and north to put some distance between him and the fighting. He led the horse rather than riding, in order to lower his silhouette and rest the exhausted animal. After several hours, the firing died out. It did not move from its original area in any direction. He knew. The fight was over and the command was lost.

Chapter 2

John continued away from the battle area, pressing more north than east now. Soon he began to see bodies of troops in blue moving away from the battle area, laughing and talking. At about four in the afternoon, he found a small wood draped over a hill, a little valley, and a stream. The foliage was thick and the wood large enough to prevent anyone from seeing deeply into its concealing shadows. In its middle, there was a tiny grassy glade beside the banks of a clear, cool stream. He led the pony into the glade and picketed it where it could get water and grass. The habits of discipline made him clean and reload his pistols and carbine, and groom and inspect his horse and equipment. When he had finished, he stripped and bathed his worn, wounded, filthy body in the little stream. At last, he stretched out on his blankets and was instantly asleep.

The jingle of harness and the clank of sabers in scabbards waked him about dawn. He listened quietly as the body of troops passed on the road, about a hundred and fifty yards away, in ground fog that lay like a healing poultice on the land. After they passed, it was silent again. His horse still stood asleep in the middle of the little glade. He dozed again until the sun rose higher and warmed him. He considered a fire and decided against it. He found some bread and cheese in his saddlebags and had a cold breakfast.

When he had finished, he began a slow, careful walk around the woods down to the edge of the road and back up to the top of the hill. At the summit he could see much of the surrounding countryside to the east and south. John studied the area where he thought the battle was fought. All seemed to be quiet except for the occasional steamboat whistle. There were occasional small bodies of troops in blue moving in different directions. Some appeared to be searching, but others were route marching away from the battle area. He decided to stay put for another day or two if he could do so without discovery. His inspection of the wood had revealed a path leading into it from the north to the stream in the little glade. That meant a possibility of unwanted visitors arriving unannounced. He decided to move up the hill to a much smaller open space that he found on the backside of the summit.

When he had moved, he gave his mount the last of the grain. He ate the rest of the bread and lay down to sleep. The sound that awakened him was girlish laughter. He quickly rolled his bedding, tied it to his saddle, and saddled his horse. When he was ready to make his escape, he moved silently down toward the sound that had awakened him.

When he could see into the glade, he flushed scarlet. Three young girls and a woman were nearly naked frolicking in the stream. He slipped backward away from the clearing. As he straightened to walk away, his shoulder touched a rotten limb and broke it. The sound of the break was soft, but the impact of the heavy branch when it hit the ground was a reverberating thump. He crouched and was still. He could see the woman look in his direction for a moment, smile, and then look away. After a minute or two passed and no one looked in his direction, he moved back to his horse and equipment.

The joyful noise had ended several hours ago. He led his horse down to water and grass at twilight. As the horse grazed contentedly, he walked along the path to see where it would take him. At the north edge of the wood, the path ran between a grain field and a pasture. On the far side lay another small wood. He started across the opening slowly and carefully. Halfway across, a shadow detached from the deeper gloom of the trees ahead of him. He crouched and drew his pistol. The shadow resolved into the shape of a woman. "Don't worry, you are in no danger," she said softly.

Her voice was clear and carried well without being loud. John stood erect but did not holster his pistol.

She walked up to him confidently. "You are a Rebel, aren't you." It was not a question.

"I am a soldier in the Provisional Army of the Confederate States of America, miss, not a Rebel."

"Well, whatever you are, you have very few friends in this country today. Morgan and all of his men were captured yesterday."

"Not all," he said softly.

"No, not all, apparently, but most have been taken and are being shipped by steamboat to prison. Do you want to go with them?"

"No, I have other things to do before this war is over."

"I am ready to help you if you want help. I know you need help. In your uniform you will be arrested and turned over to the army. You have little to eat and probably have no money that you can use to buy food. The countryside is aroused. Strangers will be noticed. Any clothes that are not in local styles will attract attention." She stopped talking and looked at him intently.

"How do you propose to help me, and why?"

"I will give you clothes and some food. I have a very little money to give you. You will have to find work to get a place to stay and food as you travel back to the South. It is a long way to country friendly to you through West Virginia. As to what I want, you must wait and see. I will be back in a little while with the clothes and money. You must wait for me in the little glade where you saw us today. Will you wait there for me? I won't be long." Her voice was soft and husky.

John nodded slowly, but he said nothing. She caught his silence and looked at him intently.

"You must do as I ask. It will be safer for you. You do not know this country and you will be caught if you try to escape alone. You will find what I want from you to be quite pleasant; besides, if you do not do as I ask, it is certain that you will be pursued and caught as more than a Rebel soldier."

The threat was implicit.

"Miss, it is not ladylike to threaten a gentleman. A lady of your beauty and breeding need never do so."

It was her turn to be silent for a long moment. Finally, she said, "I will see you shortly in the glade." She turned and walked back across the field in the gathering darkness.

John watched her out of sight before he turned and walked quietly back along the path. As soon as he was completely hidden by the darker shadows of the wood, he moved rapidly to his horse and mounted.

Chapter 3

An hour later, he was about six or seven miles northeast of the wood. He urged his rested mount to a steady ground-eating rack. Alternating this gait with the walk and short periods of leading the horse, he was well clear of his former hiding place by midnight when a nervous voice called out, "Stop where you are! Who are you?"

"Which company are you from, son?"

"Are you an officer?"

"Yes, I am down from Columbus on an inspection tour. Didn't they teach you how to challenge someone so that you stay safe?"

"No, sir, they just said for me to come on out and stop any Rebels that might have gotten away from the big battle."

"Good for you," John answered. "Now, I am going to teach you the proper way to do this job, and you can teach the man who relieves you. When a stranger approaches, first, you say, 'Halt! Who goes there!' When he stops, you say, 'Advance and be recognized!' He will walk up to you slowly and you can ask him whatever password and countersign you are using. Since I am not from the local area, I will not ask you for the one you are using. Let's just say the password is 'Abraham' and the countersign is 'Lincoln.' When the stranger gets close you say, 'Abraham.' He answers, 'Lincoln.' Then you say 'Pass, friend.' That's easy isn't it?"

"Yes, sir! Thank you, sir. I'll pass that on."

"Who is your captain, son?'

"Sam Woodward, sir. I mean Captain Woodward."

"You tell Captain Woodward that I said you did a fine job, and give him Captain McKenzie's best wishes. The people up in

Columbus are going to hear about this."

John put spurs to his horse and cantered past the young Ohio militiaman with a salute, and made fifteen miles more before he looked for a place to hide. Soon he had to find some clothes.

Two nights later, as he passed through a town after midnight, he heard snoring by the roadside. Leaning up against a stump was a drunken man. John dismounted and drew his pistol. Several nudges with a boot toe did not rouse the sleeping man, so John quickly unbuttoned the man's pants and pulled them off. He took the coat and hat. He checked the pockets and put the money that he found on the stump beside the empty whiskey bottle before he disappeared into the night.

For a week he traveled northward by short careful rides from late afternoon until about midnight. Here and there he picked up bits and pieces of clothing until he could throw away the clothes taken from the drunk and present himself as a prosperous working farmer. About ten miles north of Pittsburgh, he bought a suit of clothes that gave him the character of a man of business. He bought a pack-horse and some boxes in which to store his carbine and extra pistols instead of wrapping them into his blanket roll. In Pittsburgh, he got a bath, a haircut, and a shave before finding a rooming house owned by a respectable lady recommended by a local Methodist preacher.

Within four days, he had visited two banks and opened accounts with part of the gold that he carried. He was introduced to several men of prominence as an energetic young man recently arrived from the west with money to invest. Over the course of several weeks, he looked at several opportunities. He finally settled on two businesses. The first was an oil drilling company. The company did not buy or take leases. It hired out to drill for those who did. The management of the company demanded enough of the price from its customers up front to be insulated against losses with security for the balance. He went through the bank and an attorney to insure that his invest-ment was protected. He decided to work personally as a dealer for a smaller distillery that produced a good quality whiskey. He chose this because the chance for profit was excellent, and he could sell to the Union army down in West Virginia. He made similar arrange-ments to protect his investment in the event of his absence.

Chapter 4

John started as he recognized the man crossing the street toward him. The face was haggard and drawn, but it was unmistakably the face of Albert Goddard. John turned quickly and took an intense interest in the wares of the saddlery behind him until Goddard passed. John turned and slowly followed the man along the street, keeping well back to avoid notice and recognition. After a block or two, Albert Goddard turned into a small hotel. John crossed the street so that he could get a look at the windows of the upper floor. Shortly after Goddard entered, John saw a flash of light behind the window of the end room on the second floor. The arm that released the curtain was clad in Goddard's coat. John loitered for over an hour watching as the sun dropped slowly toward the horizon. At last, he turned and started back toward his own lodgings.

Half a block away, a slight figure, nattily dressed, stepped in front of him. "Is this Mr. McKenzie?" the man asked. Startled, John drew back and focused on his challenger's face. "Chilles? 'Chilles? What are you doing here?"

"Right now I have been following you. I saw you and was walking to meet you when I realized that you were following that man. Why were you so interested in him?"

"He is Albert Goddard, the man who identified and accused Miss Montgomery. I do not know what he is doing here, and I want to know. If I can do him any harm, I mean to do it. Let's go get something to eat and think it over. The last thing we want to do is attract the attention of civilian law to us. There is almost no military presence to worry about here."

Over supper, the two decided on a plan and went back to John's rooms to wait until the small hours of the night.

'Chilles swung his leg over the edge of the roof of the hotel porch. As soon as he was safely up, he turned and offered his arm to John below. John took the extended hand and when 'Chilles was ready, he jumped upward. 'Chilles pulled upward and gave John the extra boost necessary to grab the edge of the roof. When both were up, they slipped through an open hallway window on Albert Goddard's floor. They counted the doors until they found his door. As they expected, they found it locked. 'Chilies pulled out a screwdriver and quickly disassembled the lock. They slipped silently into the room and lifted a chair in front of the door to block it. John lighted the lamp on the table beside the still-sleeping Albert Goddard's bed. "My God!" John gasped. "He looks like a dead man."

Goddard's eyes opened. He did not appear to be startled or afraid of the two men standing over him. "Mr. Goddard, do you remember me?"

Goddard closed his eyes slowly and seemed to think before answering. "Yes, I remember you Lieutenant, or is it Captain now?"

"Do you know why we are here?"

"If you are asking if I know why you are here with me, I am sure you are angry at what I did to the beautiful girl who fooled me and our Union generals so well. As to why you are in Pittsburgh, I can say that I do not know."

"Mr. Goddard, you have caused her to be put before a court martial that had every intention of hanging her. Even though she escaped and has fled for her life, if your troops find her anywhere she will go back to trial. If you win this war, she will go back to trial. I want to make sure that you are not there to witness against her."

Goddard only sighed. "I will not be there, whatever you do, Lieutenant. I am dying. I have a cancer. I do not have much time to live. I came to Pittsburgh to see a doctor here who is studying the disease. He tells me that there is no cure and that the progress of my cancer is such that I have no more than a month or two to live. At that, the last part of that period will be filled with pain worse than what I feel now. So, you have your object without risk or danger to yourself."

'Chilles asked, "Did you make a written statement to the Union court martial or the investigators, Mr. Goddard?"

"I made no written statement before the trial. I testified under oath as to the conversation that passed between you and the lady, and I told them what I did to report the information. They offered me immunity for that and I took it, I am ashamed to say. Hanging would have spared me the pain that I now endure and the final pain which will come soon."

'Chilles was silent a moment before speaking. "Would you care to make a dying declaration of any kind, Mr. Goddard?"

Goddard smiled, but remained silent for a long time. John started to speak, but 'Chilles nudged him to silence.

Finally, Goddard spoke, "What would you expect that I might wish to say, young man?"

'Chilles deliberated before speaking. "There are several possibilities, Mr. Goddard. There is always the possibility that you now realize that you were mistaken in your identification of the young lady. You could have been mistaken as to the content of the conversation. It is possible that you might have exaggerated the remarks made by the young lady in order to gain favor and status with the Union forces."

Goddard listened. "Do you think any of those revelations would provoke a retaliation against my widow?"

"I cannot see how."

"How do you, as young as you are, know so much about the law?"

"I studied law at Princeton College before the war and practiced one year with my father who was appointed a federal judge by President Buchanan, sir."

Albert Goddard was silent for several minutes. "Are you in love with her, Lieutenant?"

"Yes, sir."

"Are you going to marry her?"

"God willing, yes, sir."

"I love my wife very much, too. I want a promise from you. If you will give me what I ask, I will make a dying declaration that will clear your loved one."

"What is it that you wish me to promise?" John asked.

"I ask that you promise to give my statement to a federal authority who can be relied upon to use it to its fullest potential to right all of the wrongs it describes and who has adequate authority to insure that such actions are carried out. Will you do that?"

"I shall do all you ask."

"Good, Lieutenant, you stay with me and send your young lawyer friend to get a lot of paper to take down my statement. It will be very long, so bring plenty of ink and paper, young man."

It was noon before they were finished. John and 'Chilles helped Albert Goddard pack his bag and took him down to the steamboat wharf. When he was settled in his cabin, they said goodbye with a warm handshake. Goddard asked one final question as they were about to leave. "Tell me who the girl really is now that the matter is settled?"

John answered, "She is Cynthia Montgomery, Major Homer Montgomery's daughter and my second cousin."

Goddard started as if he had been struck. "Homer Montgomery of Kentucky?" he stammered.

"Yes, sir."

"Thank God you found me in time!"

"Why? What do you mean?"

"My wife and Homer Montgomery were in love. Although she married me, she has always had the tenderest feelings for Homer and his late wife. If I had been the instrument of his daughter's destruction, it would have killed her. Oh, thank God. Thank God! That was the reason for my illness. It was meant to send me to meet you and to save her life. You must not fail to get that declaration in competent hands as soon as you can do so."

"Mr. Goddard, I will leave tomorrow to put it in the hands of my father in Louisville," 'Chilles reassured him.

"No! You must come with me now, and we will go together to your father and present it. Both of you must come. You must come!"

"John will be in grave danger if he goes into Louisville."

"He must come. We cannot fail. He can pose as my doctor."

Chapter 5

The three of them stayed together in Albert Goddard's cabin all the way to Louisville. At the dock, the younger men helped Goddard off the boat and hired a buggy to take them up into town. Blue uniforms were everywhere, but no one gave the trio a second glance. The federal courthouse was another matter, however. Military guards were at every entrance to the building. While 'Chilles helped Goddard down from the buggy, John watched men passing into the building. Each person was stopped and questioned. Some showed paper of some kind and others were shunted to one side to wait for some other action. As John climbed down, he beckoned 'Chilles close to him. He told him of what he had observed. 'Chilles nodded and said, "Pay the driver and make some conversation with him until I call you; then hurry directly to me and follow us into the building."

John dawdled over the payment and asked questions about local rooming houses and saloons, a subject he was sure the driver would be knowledgeable about, until he heard his name called. He thanked the driver and, clapping his hat down tight on his head, hurried to join the other two. He could hear 'Chilles remarking sarcastically about doctors who got lost between the fence and the front step. "Coming, sir, coming," he rushed to join them. 'Chilles did not wait but turned and entered the courthouse. John was ten feet behind 'Chilles and Goddard as they passed the guard. The guard stepped in front of John and barred his way with his musket.

"Where do you think you're going, mister?" growled the soldier.

Before John could answer, 'Chilles was on the man, shouting,

"Damn your eyes, you get the hell out of his way, or I will see you in a cell in that building so long you'll forget what the sun looks like. He's with me!"

The soldier went from startled to sullen. "He ain't got no pass," he snarled.

"I have the pass that covers all of us. Come on, Doctor."

"I'll shoot if he doesn't show a pass."

"Shoot and you will hang," 'Chilles tossed over his shoulder as they entered the courthouse.

It was late in the evening when they left the courthouse. Judge Wallace had read Goddard's statement carefully. He interviewed each of them separately under oath. When he was done, he had 'Chilles draft several orders and signed them. Goddard was exhausted and lay silently on a sofa in the judge's office. "Gentlemen, let me tell you what I have accomplished today.

"I have ordered the United States attorney to bring before a federal grand jury the results of an investigation that he is to conduct of the activities of the provost marshal of Lexington, Kentucky, one Colonel Anson Grimes, in relation to his dealings in property of Rebels, suspected Rebels, and others who came under his influence and power in the course of the exercise of his office. If he finds wrongdoing, he is to seek an indictment.

The judge's face was stern as he spoke. "I have ordered the general commanding at Lexington to show cause why he has arraigned before a court martial a citizen unconnected to the army who is exonerated from any offense by a dying declaration of the only witness against her. He is further to make reparations to her for her unlawful detention, the confiscation of her property on a public road, and for an assault on her by troops under his command that resulted in the homicide of her servant, and for the damage to her name and reputation caused by his unlawful acts. Damages will be appointed by this court at a future hearing. I have issued an injunction to forestall any action whatsoever by any federal authority against any party involved in the so-called espionage activities of the person known as Mary Ready or against any party thought to be a witness to that activity. I believe these orders should silence this matter and see justice done. Do you have any questions or suggestions for me? I have identified you all as interested citizens who have personal knowledge of the events without reference to your present activities, commercial or otherwise. My son is identified as a lawyer. You, Mr. McKenzie, are identified as a whiskey merchant from Pittsburgh. Mr. Goddard is a banker. All of those are correct identifications, are they not?" All nodded their agreement.

"Now, gentlemen, if you would give me a few moments in private with my son, I would be obliged. Mr. Goddard, there is another sofa in the outer office. Please use it as your condition demands. Thank you for your love of justice."

John and 'Chilles sat in the judge's outer office before leaving the building. 'Chilles was headed back south to take Albert Goddard home and then move on to get close behind the Union army in Tennessee to send information on to the Confederate Army farther south. He gave John a name and address to memorize who would be his contact in Western Maryland with the Union army there and in West Virginia on the flank of the Shenandoah. They looked out the window to see if the guard outside had changed and then helped a weak and exhausted Albert Goddard to the street and into a cab. As they left, John headed toward the steamboat landings.

Chapter 6

John had not gone more than two blocks before he discovered that he was being followed. He paused at a store window and caught the image of the burly Yankee courthouse guard behind him. His mind raced back to his arrival at the courthouse just a few hours ago to find a reason for this man's interest in him. He could think of nothing more than the peremptory treatment that 'Chilles had given the soldier at the courthouse door. The man had been humiliated in front of other members of his unit. He was probably the terror of the other soldiers and needed to re-establish his reputation for dominance. If that were the case, the voice of reason or even a bribe would probably fail to deter a confrontation. In fact, the more public the confrontation, the more the brute's reputation would be advanced. Yet a public fistfight was not in John's interest at all.

As they approached the river, John turned from the main street leading to the steamboat landing and headed for the warehouses. As his destination became obvious, he could hear the footsteps of his shadow begin to draw closer. He picked up his own pace to maintain a good distance between them. He finally found a dark passageway between a busy saloon and a shuttered building. He turned in quickly and sprinted down the pathway. At the back corner of the building, the alleyway turned to the left a few feet and then turned right again and continued on toward the next street. John dodged into the shadows on the right side at the first corner and flattened himself against the wall. He drew his big colt revolver and waited.

In seconds, the sound of footsteps told of the man's approach. As his figure came into view, John swung the heavy gun as hard as he could at the man's face. The bulky form lunged to the left, away from the blow, but the barrel gave a loud crack as it struck his forehead. John followed his first blow with a downward stroke to the side of the man's neck, but the man partially parried with an upraised right arm. He lunged forward, grabbing John around the waist and slammed him backward against the building. He felt the man release him and step back to strike with his fists. John thumbed back the hammer of his pistol and shot him in the face. The roar and flash of the shot seemed to fill the space. The soldier staggered backward and sank to his knees. John struck him again across the face and bolted on down the alley to the street beyond.

He holstered his pistol before he emerged into the faint glow of the streetlights. He turned back toward the main streets and walked deliberately but not quickly. He turned several corners to break the straight line of his route until he came to the main street. In a quarter of an hour he was at the steamboat wharf and had bought a ticket back to Pittsburgh.

Ulysses S. Grant opened the letter from the army in Kentucky. The cover was from Martin Hurlburt, his family lawyer and old friend from Ohio. The enclosure was a description of the actions of one Captain James C. Michaelman who analyzed the intentions of Morgan and helped to direct the pursuit to cut off and destroy his command.

The personal letter read:

Dear Sam,

I have enclosed a report on my intelligence officer. He has done a fine job and deserves recognition, but will get none here. Too many officers senior to him and to me are claiming the whole thing was their idea. A brevet is probably impossible, but if you could find a spot for him where his ability can be used to our advantage against the Rebels, he might get a promotion out of it. I will be sorry to lose him, but I am resigning and returning home. Beth has not been well, and I need to be there to care for her. Please give our love to Julia when you write.

Your Obedient Servant,
Martin

Chapter 7

In the fall, John took a wagonload of small kegs of good whiskey down into West Virginia to the Federal army there. He found that a cup of good whiskey was as good a pass as any paper. A small keg of his best to a brigade commander had him dining with the senior officers of the brigade. He sold first to the officers of the regiments and then to the sergeants. Then he was welcome everywhere he went. After his first visit, he was begged to return soon.

John made a trip every month. He made it his rule to not sell his whiskey in small quantities. He did not want to compete with the official sutlers or run a saloon in a tent. He sold small kegs and barrels of good quality liquor to the officers and noncommissioned officers of the army. His quality whiskey delivered by a respectable businessman commanded a good price and got access for him to the circles of power and information. He made excellent profits and accumulated a fund of firsthand knowledge about the state and plans of the army. There were many things that he did not know specifically, but he could infer many things from what he did know coupled with his own experience.

As winter began, the headquarters activity shifted back to Cumberland, Maryland. John was able to find a room in The Revere House hotel in the middle of town. The first night when he went down to supper he arrived at the door to the dining room at the same time as a fine-looking man who was wearing the shoulder straps of a major general and sporting the most luxurious side-whiskers that John had ever seen. At the door to the dining room, they almost collided as John was so focused on the whiskers.

"My goodness! I beg your pardon, General. After you, please."

The general gave him an appraising look as he made a courteous bow and stepped into the room. Both men stood looking about the room for a pleasant place to sit. "Young man, I shall have a number of my staff joining me in a moment. It seems that all other places are taken, but if you do not object, you may join us at our table by the window." He gestured to a long oval table with ten places set.

"It would be an honor to join you, sir. I am John McKenzie."

"The honor shall be ours, sir. I am George Crook. Tell me, what brings you here, Mr. McKenzie?"

"I sell whiskey to your officers and non commissioned officers, General. Only fine whiskey and in limited quantities, I must add. I would hate to contribute to any delinquency in the army. May I offer you a small keg for you and your staff?"

"Thank you, young man. I am sure that my staff would enjoy it in modest quantities, but I must decline. I have never imbibed."

"I certainly respect that, General. I am a very moderate user myself and do not miss it much when it is not available."

George Crook gave him a cool, appraising look. "Then you could not have been in the army, since it always seems to be available where troops are assembled. I have served for years in the regular army and with volunteers and have never found whiskey to be absent even when water, food, and ammunition were scarce."

The other officers joined them and were greeted by pointed remarks by the general as to his having to wait for them instead of them waiting for him. The members of the staff were intelligent, able men, and the meal passed in pleasant conversation. Many of them were Ohioans, as was George Crook, and talk was of home and of the war in general. John asked questions from time to time about war issues. He was silent when talk turned to home, as he did not want to be questioned too closely, because he would have to conceal certain details and that might trip him up later.

For a week or two he dined occasionally with the general and his military family. He gained a good knowledge of the condition of the army and more about its commander. George Crook was an intelligent, energetic, professional soldier. He was attentive to details and truly cared for his men. He was not a particularly warm man personally, but that did not mean that he did not value people as individuals. Personal friendliness was not a big factor in his relations with others. He was a formidable commander with an excellent force under his control. He would be a dangerous threat to the left flank of the Confederate forces under Jubal Early operating in the Shenandoah Valley of Virginia. While the general and his staff had been much too discreet to reveal any specific plans, the trend of the conversations, the activity of the soldiers in training, and the harassed and worn look of his quartermaster who was responsible for supplying the army would have been quite enough to reveal a move south in the spring. The stocks of food, clothing, and ordnance supplies filling the local storehouses were an exclamation point to the idea.

While this was useful information as confirmation of what might be a reasonable expectation on the part of Confederate commanders preparing to meet the threat, it was not enough to help that much. Some indication of a specific objective was needed to allow Confederate soldiers to be between the objective and the attacking blue army. There were simply never enough of the lean, hard-fighting gray infantry to guard against every possible threat.

John passed the information that he was able to gather to his local contact in code and debated with himself about ways to extract some hint of George Crook's intentions. It was out of the question to ask more than one leading question. One might be passed off as mere curiosity. More than one would attract attention. George Crook was no fool. A seasoned veteran, he always demonstrated not only an appreciation of the value of good intelligence about his opponents, but also a thorough knowledge of the background and culture of his opponents.

Crook was at a disadvantage now. In a large number of cases in this war, opposing commanders knew each other. In some cases, they had even been close friends and classmates at West Point. Both of Crook's opponents came from civil life and were unknown to him in any way. Because he did not know them, there was much more guess work about what they might do and the risks they would run in battle. He needed this information.

"Good evening, General. I see you are on time and your staff is un-punctual as usual."

Crook looked grim. "Yes, I guess I should be patient with them. They work hard, so I do not have to do so. I even need more help, so we have a new member of my staff joining us tonight. He is about your age, Captain James Michaelman. Captain Michaelman has done a fine job in Kentucky and was the man who sorted out where John Hunt Morgan was headed last year. He will be with us from here on."

John snatched his handkerchief from his pocket and coughed into it to cover his surprise. "I shall look forward to making his acquaintance, General." And I shall look for a chance to kill him if I have half a chance, he thought.

A few moments later, the staff came to the dining room more or less in a body and John was introduced to the slender captain. At the table, they sat across from each other. "Tell me Captain, where do you come from?'

"I am an Ohioan, Mr. McKenzie, just like the general. I served in an Ohio regiment and on the staff of a division in the army of the Cumberland in Kentucky and Tennessee. And you, sir, where do you come from?"

Oddly, it was a question that no one had asked John up to this moment, and many faces turned to hear an answer. He had been thinking about his answer for a good while and was ready for the question.

"I am a Kentuckian originally, now displaced by the war and the need to make a living."

"And have you served in this war, sir?"

It was a damned rude question. General Crook cleared his throat and was about to break in when John responded.

"Briefly, sir. My service was ended by enemy action."

Michaelman flushed as he realized how rude he had been and how neatly but courteously he had been put in his place.

John quickly changed the subject. "I thought I heard some wolves howling near here on one of my rides. Could that be possible?"

As the group followed his lead away from the tender subject,

John relaxed inwardly and thought to himself, Yes, boy, and every-thing I told you was gospel truth. You will be reminded of it in due course, too, if I have my way about it.

Each day George Crook sat down with Jimmy Michaelman. Their conversations covered the information of the Confederate forces and the country to the south. The efforts of the Confederates to gain information about their own army were also a part of their discussions. Crook felt sure that the town held Confederate sym-pathizers who would gladly give information, but so far they had not been able to identify anyone who actually gave information to the South. Michaelman was directed to begin to compile lists of people in a position to have valuable information and then check up on them. "Give me a partial list by the end of the week, Jimmy," Crook said.

Michaelman was a diligent worker and a clear thinker. His first task was to set down what the enemy would want to know and then list how they could find it out. He ignored the means of trans-mission of information south because he was well aware of the numbers of civilians who traveled back and forth across the lines regularly. Instead, he focused on the people in town who could collect information. He began by sorting out those who dealt with the army and had firsthand knowledge of facts. His list of contrac-tors and sutlers named over a hundred people. He decided to plow through the list, starting with the ones who provided food and transportation to the army as they would have firsthand knowl-edge of the strength and movement plans days in advance of actual movement.

Chapter 8

Two weeks later, John was late for the evening meal. As he entered the dining room, he saw that the general's table was full and there was a young woman seated on his right between him and Captain Michaelman. It was not Mary Deakin, the hotel owner's daughter, whom most knew had caught the general's eye. John chose a table across the room with one of the last seats available. The meal passed pleasantly until the young woman turned and looked to her right so that she was in profile.

My God, it is her, he thought. There could be no mistake. It was the girl from the stream in Ohio. He hardly tasted the rest of his food and responded only occasionally to the conversation at his table. There was very little that he could do. She would recognize him, certainly. Her choices would be to identify him immediately or pretend that she did not know him because of the compromising circumstances of their meeting. As the group rose from the table, he knew the next few moments would determine whether he was to be hanged as a spy or not.

The general took her on his arm with James Michaelman following them. Their way led them toward John's table on the way out of the dining room. She saw John across the room and flushed. General Crook caught his eye and motioned to him. John stood and excused himself from his dinner companions.

"Miss Adams, May I present Mr. McKenzie. Mr. McKenzie is a frequent companion of ours at the table and a purveyor of excellent whiskey, so my staff tells me."

Eve smiled. "Why, General, this is a pleasant surprise. Mr. McKenzie and I met briefly some time ago when he stopped at our farm for refreshment on his travels. He did not stay as long as we would have liked, but I am sure that his business was very pressing."

"Why, yes, miss, it was very pressing at the time, but perhaps now I can make up for the past."

"Miss Adams is Captain Michaelman's fiancée, Mr. McKenzie. They are to be married at the end of the month, so you will have very little time to spend in conversation. Make the most of it, sir. I am sure that Captain Michaelman will monopolize every moment he can of this beautiful lady's time."

John bowed as they walked past and met a penetrating gaze from Michaelman as he straightened.

"Congratulations, Captain. She is a most charming lady. You are a fortunate man, sir."

Michaelman did not smile. He only nodded.

"Well, well," John murmured to himself. As he followed the three out of the dining room, he thought, He knows or suspects that she is at least a flirt, or he is just a very jealous man. But now I know about when they will move. Whatever action I can take will have to happen by the end of the month or shortly afterward.

There was no sleep that night for John. He spent the night working out his plan and encoding it.

By the next afternoon, it was in the hands of Lieutenant McNeill and his partisan Rangers to the south of Cumberland in the mountains.

Chapter 9

The mare paced lightly over the icy patches on the road west out of Cumberland. She was sleek and full of energy after more than a year of light use and good feed. Her joy in the cold air and the opportunity to stretch her legs without the company of other horses was evident in the toss of her head and the spring in her step.

John saw the man that he had been told to expect, standing by his mount inspecting its hooves as if something might be the matter. He reined the mare to a walk as he approached the man. The man came erect and faced John with his eyes fixed on John's own eyes.

"Do you have some trouble?" John launched into the recognition code.

"I think my horse may be lame."

"What made you think he was lame?"

"He stumbled a lot. He is not used to all this cold weather."

"Neither am I," John completed the code.

"Tell me about the number, strength, and location of the picket posts, where the generals sleep, and anything else you can think of that we need to know."

"Do you want to get out of the road, Mr. Fay? This is going to take a while."

"No names, please. No, if someone saw us leaving the road or returning it might attract unwanted notice. I will ride with you farther west until you finish. Then you can turn back to town. There will be someone behind us who will give us warning if someone from Cumberland comes along behind us."

As they rode slowly westward, John detailed all that he knew about the current arrangements of the Union army in and around Cumberland. He warned the messenger that the location on the roads of the picket posts sometimes changed, but certain roads from the east, south, and west were always guarded. When the man repeated the information and showed that he understood the meaning of it, he started to put spurs to his horse and move away from John.

"There's one more thing. I'm going south with you."

The man reined his mount to a halt and stared at John. "Why?"

"I am already compromised. There is a woman here who knows that I am a Confederate officer. She has said nothing that I know of so far, but I cannot trust that she will not let something slip in an unguarded moment or deliberately reveal what I am."

"The longer she waits to do so, the more complicit she becomes in your offense," the man said. "It will be difficult and more dangerous to her to do such a thing later than immediately. Why did she not expose you on sight?"

"I do not know why. She is a strange, passionate creature whose motivations are not those of ordinary or conventional women."

"You think she fancies you?" He was matter of fact in is tone.

"Yes, but she is engaged to a Union captain who is one of their intelligence officers. She could merely speculate about me. That would plant enough doubt in his mind to get sufficient suspicion aroused to make my work impossible, if nothing more. If she were to accuse me of improper advances, the man would be able to make short work of me. In that case, our network would crumble. If I go out with you, there is only one spy who set up this entire operation and that spy, me, has gone with his mission accomplished. The other parts of the network remain undiscovered."

"Why do you tell me this? I have no authority to approve it or forbid it."

"I want you to take a good look at this mare and make sure that she is saddled and brought out with the horses for the generals from the stable that I told you about. Will you promise to see to it?"

J. B. Fay looked over the pretty animal standing quietly beside his horse. She was certainly something that a man could care a lot for, and he knew better than John that good horseflesh was getting much harder to find in the South than it used to be. "All right, you shall have her if the situation at the moment allows. Good luck to you, Lieutenant. We will see you tonight."

"One other thing must happen."

"What is that?" Fay asked.

"The captain to whom the woman is engaged must come out as a prisoner also."

"What is this foolishness?" He was angry and it showed.

"It is not foolishness, and it is not personal other than in a remote way. The captain has identified and charged with spying a person who assisted us in deceiving the Federals back in 1862. He captured her and held her prisoner. She was on trial for her life for helping us, but she escaped. He must be put where he can do her no harm until the war is over."

"All right, I will have a mount for him too, but we concentrate on the Yankee generals. You find this captain and bring him to us. Otherwise he is your responsibility. Agreed?"

Fay gave a loud whistle and set his horse in motion westward. A rattle of hoofs sounded coming from the east, and a stocky man on a big bay horse galloped by John and joined Fay.

"How does it look, J. B.?" The stocky man asked.

"It looks pretty good. Let me tell it to you as we go so that both of us will know if we run into something on the way. We have a long way to go to meet Lieutenant McNeill."

After a hard ride, Fay rejoined his own party of men, and C. R. Hallar, the stocky man, rode back to intercept Lieutenant McNeill and guide his party into the rendezvous.

When McNeill's men and horses had rested and the plan for the raid was reviewed with tasks assigned, they set out. They rode over a long ridge and crossed a creek, then moved northward over a mountain. Here the snow had accumulated and the riders had to dismount and lead their horses through the deep snow. After a long and difficult march, the command descended to the Potomac and crossed into Maryland far behind the schedule that was to have put them into Cumberland long before this.

On the north bank Lieutenant McNeill spat reflectively into the snow as his men rubbed down their horses. "Pass the word for officers and sergeants to come on up here."

Chapter 10

In Cumberland, John finished his preparations. He had written to his bank five days earlier to transfer all of his current funds and those that came to him from his investments to an account in England that belonged to his mother. Another letter went to his attorney in Pittsburgh that instructed him to notify both companies in which he had an interest to pay him through the attorney, as he would be out of the country. The attorney was to deposit the funds in John's local bank account. He wrote a bill of sale for his remaining whiskey to the hotel with his thanks for their hospitality and in full payment for his meals and lodging. His saddlebags were packed, and he put on his uniform and weapons. All of these letters had been mailed yesterday and were on their way. At 1 AM he put on the long gray cloak that he had purchased for the winter. With his saddlebags over his shoulder, he quietly left the room and headed down the street to get Captain Michaelman.

He planned to wait outside until he saw the raiding party come in from the northwest road and then go in to take Michaelman. He did not want to be too far ahead of their arrival and, in so doing, give Michaelman the chance to sound an effective alarm.

After a full hour of waiting, doubts filled his mind, and he began to consider alternatives to the plan. He knew that he was compromised now or would be in the near future. He could not take the general by himself. Michaelman knew the plan of the army and was moderately valuable in and of himself. If something had caused the raiders to call off their effort to capture the generals, he could still make his escape and bring out Michaelman. If McNeill and his Rangers were not coming in to get the horses, he would have to go and get the horses before taking Michaelman prisoner.

He headed for the livery stable at a fast walk.

He found the stable dark and shut as he expected. He lit a lantern and saddled his mare. He picked a big, strong gelding that he had seen perform and saddled it for Michaelman. He also got a coil of rope to tie the captured man into the saddle. As he finished, he led out the horses and shut up the barn.

Lieutenant McNeill was impatient. "Boys, we're way behind time. It's going to take too long to go around the town to the unguarded road into Cumberland on the northwest. We have to go in from the east. We already know about where the Yankee pickets are, at the railroad station and at Brady's Mill. We can surprise them and go straight in."

After a moment of stunned silence, several voices objected.

"There's 'bout eight thousand blue bellies in this area. They are in the town and between us and home. Sheridan is at Winchester, and New Creek has a big garrison too. They are closer to Moorefield than we are. This ain't going to work."

"I hear what you are saying, but listen to me. This all depends on us getting through the two lines of pickets without setting off the alarm. Let's try it. If a picket gives the alarm, we can get back across the Potomac and into the hills before the Yanks can close in on us."

There was a long silence. Then a few bold souls said, "Come on, boys let's catch us a damn Yankee general or two." There was a laugh and the officers walked back to their commands calling out for the men to tighten cinches and mount up.

McNeill called out, "Vandiver, you ride with me on the point. Kuykendall, you and Fry follow us close. Welton, you keep the rest of the men closed up and tight behind us. We have about an hour and a half 'til dawn. We need to move along."

The Union vidette was located at the mouth of a ravine that carried the road up to a plateau and into Cumberland. He saw the approaching column and brought his carbine up and stepped out into the road to challenge the approaching troops. His challenge rang out and was answered by a reply, "Friends from New Creek."

The vidette then directed the column to halt and send one man forward to give the countersign. Lieutenant McNeill clapped his spurs to his horse and lunged forward directly at the bewildered sentinel. He fired his pistol into the face of the man as his horse, with the bit in his teeth, ran past. Vandiver and Fry pounced on the startled soldier and shoved their pistols into his ribs as Kuykendall led a party to overcome the lone sentinel's support of two sleepy men huddled in their blankets about a hundred yards on down the road in a fence corner. A party of swearing Confederates quickly cut off their brief attempt at flight.

The frightened Union soldiers were separated and questioned to try to discover the password and countersign. When they remained silent, a cocked pistol was pressed against the forehead of the man judged to be the most frightened of the three.

"Give me the password and countersign, Yank, or you are a dead man," McNeill threatened. Steely eyes glared at the man with no hint of mercy or forbearance. Eternity yawned.

"Bulls, Gap." It was barely a whisper.

The pistol muzzle did not waver nor did the eyes for a very long time. "He ain't lyin'" said a voice. The big revolver dropped slowly and the hammer was let down gently. The three Union soldiers were disarmed and told to sit down in their fence corner and remain there until the column re-passed them. Someone would be watching.

Amid much muttering about the damned fool business of firing a pistol when they were trying to surprise the garrison, Lieutenant McNeill got the men mounted again. Fry insisted that he and Kuykendall take the lead to the next picket so that there would be no more shooting.

The column covered the mile between the two posts quickly and closed upon the second picket. When the challenge was given, Fry answered the challenge and Kuykendall called out loudly not to crowd up so that he could give the sentinel the countersign. The misdirection gave the Confederates the extra seconds needed to close on the six men and capture them without firing a shot. Once again, the pickets were disarmed and instructed to remain where they were until the Confederates returned. They were told that they would be watched. McNeill halted a short distance along the road and called out two squads of ten men each under Kuykendall and Vandiver. These men were sent on the mission of taking the two Yankee generals into custody. Fay was to cut the telegraph lines out of the city to slow pursuit after the capture of the two generals. The final plans given, the gray troopers rode on into Cumberland.

At the Barnum House, the sentinel paced back and forth dutifully, with his mind more devoted to keeping warm than to paying attention to the cavalry scouting party coming in to report. The first man to dismount walked over to the sentry and, drawing his pistol, made him a prisoner without the least fuss or disturbance. The man was quick to tell the raiders where on the second floor the general slept. The men filed quietly into the hotel and up the stairs to the designated room. The occupant turned out to be General Kelley's adjutant. Awakened from a sound sleep, he answered the question about the whereabouts of the general without thinking or caring who was asking. Kelley was awake instantly and hurried to dress under the watchful eyes of the Confederates. As soon as he was clothed, he and his adjutant were hustled down to the street and each mounted double in front of a trooper.

Down the street at the Revere House, the identical scene was played out.

"General Crook, you are my prisoner!"

"By whose authority?"

"By the authority of General Rosser of Fitzhugh Lee's Cavalry Division."

"Is General Rosser here?"

"I am General Rosser," Vandiver lied, "and the whole town is taken."

"Then I am your prisoner."

The group of riders came out of the darkness as John led the horses away. Three of them peeled off from the group and headed him off. One of them asked, "Can we help you with those horses, sir?"

"Is your officer Lieutenant McNeill?"

"Yes, sir," after a pause.

"I am Lieutenant McKenzie and these are two of the horses you are looking for. I thought you were not coming. I am going to get the other man that we are looking for. I will meet you in front of the Revere House in a few minutes."

John opened the front door quietly and stepped softly up the stairs. At the door he listened for a moment and then opened it. He closed the door behind himself and let his eyes adjust to the darkness. He went to the window and opened the curtains to let in the moonlight. He was startled to see two figures in the bed. He crept to the bedside and bent low to whisper in Michaelman's ear.

"Captain, Captain! The general needs you immediately. Please dress for a ride and hurry. I am sorry to disturb you. I will wait outside in the hall."

"Yes. I'll be along in a moment." He was still half asleep and did not recognize John's voice.

John could hear the stirrings in the room, some soft conversation, and then the door opened. Without a word, John led the way down the stair and out the front door. Michaelman was still dressing and mumbling to himself as he mounted. As he took his seat in the saddle he asked, "Where did you get this iron-mouthed nag, soldier?"

For the first time, he looked directly at John. "What the hell are you doing here? What is this all about?"

"Captain Michaelman, allow me to properly introduce myself. I am Lieutenant John McKenzie, Provisional Army of the Confederate States of America. You, sir, are my prisoner."

"The hell you say!"

John McKenzie drew an army colt and cocked it. The metallic click of the sear engaging the hammer on the pistol was a clear and precise admonition for compliance. "Walk your horse to the hotel, Captain."

The generals were mounted at the head of the column, and the Rangers fell into a military column formation. The flags of General Crook and General Kelley were unfurled and the column moved east out of town at a brisk trot.

At each outpost, the party galloped through with flags flying and shouts to make way for General Crook and General Kelley. Union soldiers saluted as the captured generals thundered past.

By the time the raiders crossed the river, the Union army had recovered from its surprise.

"You are not going to escape us," Michaelman shouted at John.

"We will see about that, Captain. The day and the hunt are not over yet."

"Sheridan is close by to the east at Winchester; he is as close to Moorefield as we are, and he has fresh horses and troops. He will cut us off in plenty of time."

"Perhaps he can cut off part of the party, Captain, but you and I will escape him on our own, if it comes to that."

"Why me? I thought at first when I recognized you tonight that it had to do with Eve. But, if that were what it was, you would not have come with us. Two generals and two captains only? The captains do not make sense."

"Keep your mount closed up to the man in front of you, Captain Michaelman."

John looked back to his left, and he could see in the distance the shadowy mass of the head of a column of horsemen. He knew that they were not friendly. The river was between the Confederate raiders and the pursuing Union riders. The danger would be at the bridges and fords up stream. If the pursuers could catch and pass the Confederates and their prisoners, they could cross the stream and force the party to disperse at best, and at worst, to stand and fight against a superior force that was constantly being reinforced.

Lieutenant McNeill dropped back along the column to the body of men following John and Captain Michaelman.

"I want you men to start shooting at them as you ride when they catch up with us. At the first bridge, about three miles ahead, stop and fight them if they are close. I think they will try to cross. If you fight and delay them as long as you can, they will see that we are getting back our lead. They will break off the fight and try to keep up. Remount and keep up with them at least to the next bridge about five miles farther on. After that, keep up if your horses can do it. If not, meet us on the mountain tomorrow. Lieutenant McKenzie, keep your prisoner with the two generals. If we are forced to break up, that group will split off with a guide and small escort. The rest of the company will stand long enough to let you get away to the Valley."

In Richmond, Jimmy Michaelman was marched to Libby Prison. Outside, an officer and several guards went through the group of captured Union officers searching them while they were told the rules of the prison. That screening done, they were let into the white-washed, former warehouse. One of the guards told them, "Best you find men of your own unit or state to settle down with. Prisoners ain't friendly to strangers."

Jimmy asked where Ohio was, and he was directed up to the next floor. The Ohio officers questioned him briefly and then took him to meet the senior officer. After telling him his story, he got right to the point. "How do we get out of here?" The colonel laughed and told him that he was a year too late. Just about a year ago, Colonel Abel Streight and 108 others had tunneled out and escaped to Union lines at Fortress Monroe. Since then, the guards had been much more careful and escape was nearly impossible.

In the long days of watching and waiting, Jimmy Michaelman learned a lot. He learned the importance of food to strength and spirit in men. He learned to fight off despair with action. He paced the walls on every floor. He measured and calculated, but in the end, he had to wait for the resumption of prisoner exchanges.

Book Four

The Bitternees of Gall and the Taste of Honey

Chapter 1

John waited in the dugout in the trench wall outside of Petersburg. The lean infantry captain finished talking to his sergeant. "The outposts are ready for the exchange column. Don't worry, Captain, we have been doing this frequently for a long time. Generally, the Yanks don't bother us much on exchange days until the exchanged prisoners are out of the area. I recommend that you just follow the column until you get about a mile back. There is a clearing that the exchange agents use to stop and sort the men out. Most of them have sorted themselves out as well as they can before they leave the wharf at City Point. I expect that most of your men will already be together. They will not be in very good shape, and marching will be hard for them. They have been fed poorly, and lots of them are sick. Don't be surprised."

"I have heard that and have seen some of the people who came back to us recently. We are having a better time back at Lynchburg than you are here. There are not so many of us, and there are good farms nearby that haven't been damaged by the fighting. Horses and equipment are our problem."

"Captain, they are coming in!"

John blinked at the bright March sunshine after the shadows of the earthen shelter. His eyes took in the ragged column of scarecrows marching up to the Confederate works from the Union lines across the open vale. The exchanged prisoners were scrawny and pale. Their clothes were worn out and even more of a hodgepodge than was the norm in that army that never had enough of anything but courage and fighting spirit.

"Hey, Lieutenant! Boys, Lieutenant McKenzie is a captain now."

"George, won't you ever learn to keep quiet in ranks?"

"Not today, Captain. The sergeant, Jack, and I, and ten others are here. We got all of what's left of Company B here together."

"March on ahead, and we will divide everybody up in the woods about a mile back."

When they got to Lynchburg, they had time to talk while the men were given such arms and uniforms as could be found.

"When do you think Harry Montgomery will be exchanged?" John asked.

The sergeant was silent for a long moment. He cleared his throat. "We don't know for sure, Captain. The officers were all sent to other camps, so we don't know for sure about any of them. We heard things from time to time. We heard that he did not make it."

"Did you hear what happened?"

"We heard it after the first winter. He got sick. We don't know any more or even if that is true," he added lamely.

"How did such information get from camp to camp?" John was puzzled.

"There was a man in the Second Kentucky that the Yanks thought was an officer. He didn't try to tell them otherwise. They found out and sent him to Camp Douglas. He tried to tell us everything that he could remember about our officers.

"It was pretty bad, sir. The food that we got was bad and not near enough. There were no clothes to speak of to replace our worn out uniforms and boots. When the first winter came, a lot of the boys got sick and died. Mostly, they died if they got real sick. There were twenty-two of us captured during that day and the next. We've got thirteen now. At that, we did better than most. If it had not been for the guard sergeant's dog, we would have lost two or three more."

"Dog?" John was startled.

"We were starving. Some of us were about to just give up and die. We needed meat, and we couldn't get any. There was a big Yankee sergeant that had a big black dog that he used to threaten the prisoners. Jack and George stole some tobacco from one of the civilians who worked in the camp. They traded it for some rope and a soup bone. At noon the dog was left outside while the Yank went in to stuff his belly. Jack walked close to him with the bone in his pocket. The dog smelled it and followed him around the corner of the next barracks. Jack dropped the bone into a box with a hole big enough for the dog's head. When the dog put his head in to get the bone, they snared him with the rope. We cooked him and ate him and made soup with the bone. There was enough meat on that big dog to last us all nearly five days. It gave us the extra strength to last to the warm weather."

"I don't know what to say."

"That ain't the best part, sir."

"What could be better than that?"

"We wrote a poem and tacked it to the guardroom door without getting caught. It said,

For want of bread, your dog is dead.

For want of meat, your dog we eat.

"The blue bellies tried for a month to find out who did it, but they never could find out because we never bragged about it in camp. If they had caught us, they would have killed us on the horse or something worse."

Chapter 2

The April rain and low clouds smothered the landscape and washed away men's spirits. The news of the war was all bad lately. Desertion and absence without leave had become a problem in some units. The quality of everything the army was issued had declined.

General Basil Duke looked over the officers assembled in his headquarters. "Gentlemen, as you know, a few days ago I told you that with the two hundred men that we have recently gotten in the exchange of prisoners, the brigade numbers about six hundred men. General Echols has succeeded General Early. He received and passed on to us orders to our brigade and the other units here to move east to join General Lee. General Lee was moving out of the lines around Petersburg. I must now tell you with the deepest feeling that General A. P. Hill was killed in battle at the head of his corps. This is a great loss to us, but there is much worse news to tell. We have just received word that General Lee has surrendered."

A groan of physical pain came from the men.

Duke motioned for silence. "We will now move in the direction of Danville to see if we can join General Joseph E. Johnston in North Carolina. We will move out tomorrow. I have procured as many mules as I can to mount us until we can get our horses back from Lincolnton down in North Carolina. I believe the horses will be in very good condition from rest and good grazing out of the way of the war.

"That is all, gentlemen. Captain McKenzie, will you remain with me for a moment?

"John, the infantry brigades have all but disbanded on this news. The men have laid down their arms and are deserting in droves. I want you to take your most reliable men and move about the town in a body showing your discipline and organization. More than that, I want you to collect all of the good quality arms and ammunition that you can find from those units and bring them back here so that we can be sure that our men have the best we can give them."

The cursing was eloquent, loud, and angry. John turned his horse down the side road to find out the cause of the obvious anger and frustration. He found the sergeant standing in the road facing a big mule whose ears were laid back and whose teeth were bared in menace. The mule's feet were splayed and dug into the road surface in an attitude of utter defiance.

"Captain, we got to get some horses. We can't do a damned thing with these worthless critters. They will plod down a road with the best of them, but if you hear a gunshot a mile away, they will have you in the next county. They won't charge most times, and when they do, you can't stop them 'til you are through the enemy line and got to fight your way out again while you beat the mule with the reins. You ever try to shoot and beat at the same time, Captain?"

Had the subject and the situation not been so serious, John would have burst out laughing. This was the longest speech John had ever heard from his sergeant. The volume and emotion betrayed the sergeant's feeling about the nearly hopeless task set for them.

"Don't shoot him yet, Sergeant. We are due to get most of our horses back in Lincolnton. They have wintered west of there and are coming to meet us. We have a job to do protecting President Davis from the Yankee cavalry. You know how hard they have pressed us. We can expect them to try to get ahead of us, to try to penetrate and cut our column, and to try to make us stand and fight so they can send more troops around us to close on the President while they grind us down. One more day."

"Captain, the Yanks are in Lincolnton. We can see them."

"Gallop back to General Duke and tell him. We will hold here as the column passes left or right, but we need some more men to give him time to get by. Tell him also that there is a small road we passed about a mile back coming in from the left that a local told me leads to the main road to Charlotte."

"Yes, sir!"

"Get goin', son! Sergeant, get the men spread out along that low rise and pull the horses back. Have about ten men march back and forth showing their heads and musket muzzles intermittently to give the Yanks the idea that we have infantry too!"

Within minutes the muskets began to pop as the Union cavalry came tentatively out of Lincolnton. They took some casualties right away as the long Enfield muskets of Duke's cavalry outranged the repeating carbines that the blue troopers carried. The superior numbers of the Union army began to tell. Their line got longer and denser until they began a rush. Duke's reinforcement arrived just in time, and the increased volume of Confederate fire stopped them cold. In only twenty minutes, a messenger arrived to tell John that the column had cleared marching east. He was ordered to disengage and act as rearguard.

"Fours forward with the horses. Keep them below the ridgeline. Twos and threes, fire and move back to mount, but reload and do not mount."

"They saw us move, Captain; here they come!"

"Twos and threes, back to the line and give them two rounds of aimed fire, then come back and mount. Ones, give them three rounds and then come back and mount. We got to teach them not to crowd us too close!"

In two days, they had met Dibrell's brigade with President Davis and picked up Ferguson's brigade of Mississippi cavalry. The next day they were on the road south again. The Union cavalry pressed them hard. There were scores of short, vicious little fights at crossroads and bridges as the men of Basil Duke's brigade fended off the pursuit of President Jefferson Davis as he rode south to try to join General Dick Taylor and Nathan Bedford Forrest. Davis wanted desperately to have an army and a government to continue the fight from the Deep South or the southwest.

Blue coats would press in on the small parties of gray. Gunfire. Charge and counter charge with men down and horses killed and injured. The pressure was often too much to recover their fallen men. The strength of the brigade gradually eroded. The fighting spirit of the beleaguered horsemen began to change from élan to grim determination not to be beaten. A willingness to stand and fight changed into a desire to fight to the death wherever a battle was joined. This ferocity backed off the Union troopers who knew that the end was in sight and wanted to live to see it. They followed closely and maintained contact but lunged hard and in force less frequently at the retreating column. It was as wolves follow a wounded stag just out of range of antlers and slashing hooves.

In Georgia, the Confederate President and a small party separated from his escort to travel less conspicuously when they received word that Dick Taylor and Bedford Forrest had probably surrendered. Although a few members of his party were able to evade capture, his effort to break contact with the pursuing troops failed as they saturated the roads south.

Chapter 3

General Duke's face was as worn as John had ever seen it. This normally forceful, able man looked gloomy and worn out. He was no worse looking than the officers who faced him. Arms still bright and functional did not excuse dirty uniforms and unshaven faces. He faced his officers and began to speak.

"Gentlemen, I have just met with General Breckinridge, the Secretary of War. We have done all that we can do to assist the escape of President Davis. Most of you do not know that he left the column with a small party at the time when you were all paid. He felt that he could travel in secrecy and with greater speed with a smaller party. General Breckinridge informs me also that he has good reason to believe that both General Taylor and General Forrest have surrendered. His brother, Colonel Breckinridge, and his regiment have also surrendered. The Secretary believes that even if you reach the Mississippi and cross it, you will find the Confederate forces there prepared to surrender, too. He counsels an immediate surrender. It would be folly to think of holding out longer, and it would be criminal to risk the lives of the men who have served so faithfully when no good could possibly be accomplished. He wishes that you return to your homes peacefully.

"Go and form your men and tell them what I have told you. They have striven to do their duty and preserve their honor throughout this long war. I believe they will accept without disgrace release from a service which they have so worthily discharged.

"Captain McKenzie, please come back to see me as soon as you have completed your duty to your men! Dismissed, gentlemen.

You leave with my respect and affection, as do every one of your soldiers. It will be hard for us. But we will endure that with the same courage and resourcefulness with which we have fought."

"General, I have delivered your message. I am at your orders."

"I think, John, that it would be a good idea for you to not surrender because of your activities behind the enemy lines. We do not know what they will do. The terms that have been repeated to me that were offered to General Lee and General Johnston are fair and generous. But I do not know what the Federals will do about those who have been engaged in activities other than service in the army or navy. Several Union officers know you as a spy, two of whom are generals who have been exchanged. I suggest that you make your way home without surrendering or giving your parole or that you do so under a false name."

"I think that is good advice, General, and I thank you for thinking of my particular problem when there are so many grave decisions for you to make."

"In the event that you need to leave the country, John, do you have funds?"

"Yes, General, while I was selling whiskey to the Yankees, I made nice profits in addition to collecting information. I deposited the funds in a bank and had them transferred to an account in England. By the way, some of that money on deposit is the remainder of the gold that I was given for buying information before the capture of most of our men. What should I do with it?"

"Selling whiskey to the Yankees!" The old flash and fire came back to Basil Duke's face as he threw back his head and laughed. "How much did you make? No! Don't answer the question. Bless my soul, John McKenzie, they can never beat us completely as long as we have men like you. The money? Keep it, and go find Homer Montgomery's daughter and spend it on her. If you don't do that, the Yankees will get it, and there's no guarantee that the United States Government would ever see it."

When John returned to the company, they had already begun to disperse. By twos and threes the men drifted off to the west or north, depending on where they had come from or where they thought life might be bearable after a long and bitter war.

Jack, George, and the sergeant were still waiting when John left the general. "Captain, we waited for you. We wanted to know if you would ride home with us or if you were going to do something else. George and I thought about goin' to Tennessee first to see our Grandpa, but the sergeant wants to head right for Texas. What do you think we ought to do?"

"When was the last time your families heard from you or you from them?" McKenzie asked.

"We guess they knew that we got captured, but I don't guess they know we were exchanged. None of us have gotten a letter in several years."

This statement hit John like a blow. No letters in several years. No word. No hint of who was alive or how they fared from either the soldiers or their families. What an ordeal. And I do not know if the beautiful woman whom I love lives, is in peril, or is beyond the reach of earthly harm.

"Let's go home to Texas, boys. There's one thing you have to know, all of you, before we ride together. While you were in the Yankee prison camps, I was behind their lines working as a spy. The terms of the surrender protect ordinary soldiers. They give me no protection as a spy. If I am recognized and caught, it might go hard for anybody with me. I want you to know that before you decide to do anything."

"We stuck with you through some pretty good fights, Captain. If the Yankees ain't had enough, yet, we can fix them right up."

Chapter 4

The Texas sun was already hot in late May when the four riders came to the creek south of town. They watered their horses and groomed them. Each uniform was brushed and shaken as free of the dust of the road as it could be. They rode into town at a trot right up the main street. Although returning soldiers had become an ordinary sight over the past month, these men did not ride in as though they had been beaten. They attracted attention from people on the street. At the main intersection, the order to halt was given, and the officer turned his mount to face the three soldiers who stood in a rank behind him.

"God bless you all, men. You have done all that your country demanded of you and more. You are released to go to your homes with your honor intact. Goodbye and good luck!"

The three saluted and received John's salute in return, and then all shook hands and turned their mounts toward their homes.

Cynthia was putting flowers in a tall vase in the hall. The fresh smell of the greenery and the fragrance of the blooms made her happy for a moment. The long months of waiting for some word of whether John was alive or dead had worn down her courage, and gloom settled on her too often. She heard a step on the porch of the house and looked out of the door from the darkness of the hall. A soldier stood silhouetted as so many had in the last month. Men worn out and hungry, walking home from as far away as Virginia, the Carolinas, and Tennessee. There had been released prisoners of war coming home from New York and Ohio and Illinois. They were the saddest of all. Hollow-eyed and lacking stamina, they often fell beside the road and were brought in by other returning soldiers. The churches in town had worked to give them all a helping hand along the road or to bury those who did not make it the whole way to their homes.

But the shadowed figure did not look worn out. He was lean, but carried himself at a balance. He had a tilt to his head that looked...

"John? Oh, John? Is that you?" The flowers were scattered from the hall table to the doorway as she ran to meet him. His strong strides crossed the porch and met her rush at the door. He grabbed her body and nearly crushed her in an embrace that carried love and desperate longing in it. She clung to him with all of her might and buried her face on his breast, drinking in the scent and taste of him. She sobbed and cried for joy, and he spoke to her in the growl of desire. Neither listened to the other but both knew all that was being said.

A voice full of apprehension called from the head of the stairs. "Cynthia, what is the matter? Are you all right? Who is there?"

"He's home."

"I'm home."

"He's safe."

"I am here, Mama." John's voice cracked with emotion, but the voices made a joyful chorus.

Chapter 5

It was a week after the wedding when the Union officer appeared on the front porch. He had a squad of cavalry that dismounted in the front and back of the house. He knocked loudly on the door and paced impatiently until someone came to answer his knock. Mrs. McKenzie came to see what the caller wanted when the servant fetched her.

"Yes, what is it that you want?"

"Is this the house of John McKenzie?" the blue officer asked bluntly.

"Senior or Junior, young man?" She fixed her gaze on the button of his uniform blouse just below his chin. She was a tall woman and could easily have looked him in the eye with a level gaze.

"He would be in his mid twenties...miss." He moderated his tone a bit.

"Why do you seek him, who are you, and what is your authority?" Her eyes never wavered from his top button.

He coughed and with a casual air touched his top button, as he removed his hand from his mouth. "I am Captain James Michaelman, and he is sought by a warrant issued by the military governor of this state for spying against the United States of America."

"Nonsense." She still held her gaze on the button and showed no agitation at all.

"Madame, your opinion on this legal matter carries no weight at all. I have been ordered to take him and I propose to do it today."

"Then you had better go find him. He is not here."

"Where is he?"

"I have no exact knowledge of that."

"I will search the place for him."

"Do you have a search warrant?"

"I have an arrest warrant."

"It is not the same."

"I'll do what I please to you damned Rebels."

John's mother's strong face was set. The gray eyes still bored into his button. "Young man, your youth would excuse your boorish behavior, but your uniform calls upon you for a higher standard of behavior. Your language is offensive, and your behavior is a disgrace to your organization and to your family. You have asked me questions that I have answered truthfully and specifically to the best of my knowledge. You have made an accusation against me and my household for which you have only supposition and your own prejudices as a basis.

"If you wish to search my house, go and get a warrant, present it, and you will be allowed entry. If you wish to find Mr. John McKenzie, you had better look farther afield than here. Now if you have nothing more to offer, I bid you good day. You can show yourself out."

She turned and walked out of the room. Michaelman stood rooted to the floor. He was torn between embarrassment and rage. Finally, he stamped out of the house and set four men to watch the house from front and back.

A week later, he pulled the watchers off of their posts and went back to Dallas, fuming.

When three months had passed with no hint of success in his search, he got a letter. The letter was written in a crabbed hand by someone without much writing skill. It said, *"If yu want to find Mckensie, come to Witts mill on the trinity river satday night just after sundown. Come alon."*

Michaelman's spirits shot up. He ordered a detail to watch the mill from then until Saturday night around the clock from the bluff above. Each day they reported no unusual activity. On Saturday, he rode down to the bluff and watched it himself. He posted ten cavalrymen about a hundred yards back where they could hear his whistle or any shots and ride to his support instantly.

He spent the entire night at the mill. He saw no one.

The next morning he dismissed his detail and went back to his hotel to rest before starting his Sunday routine. When he walked into his room, he was cracked across the back of his head with a pistol barrel and tripped. Strong hands caught his collar and kept him from falling heavily to the floor. Before his head cleared, he was bound and gagged and thrown onto his bed. Half a pitcher of water was poured on his face, but he could not see his assailant for a blindfold secured over his eyes.

A voice that he did not recognize asked him, "Do you know Eve Adams?"

He nodded his aching head.

"Are you married to her?"

He was silent, his mind racing, until he felt a pistol muzzle grind into his groin. He nodded, yes.

"Do you want to see her hang as a Rebel spy?"

The shock was physical. It needed no prodding from outside. He shook his head, no.

"There are four affidavits sworn and signed by persons of reputation in Ohio and Maryland to the effect that she aided and abetted a Confederate spy, one John McKenzie, in spying on the Union forces and in the abduction of two general officers of the United States Army. Certified copies have been made, and several packages have been prepared for dispatch to the Federal courts having jurisdiction over Ohio, Maryland, and Texas as well as the provost marshal general of the United States army in Washington. Another packet will be mailed to Major General George Crook. Even if the federal courts do not act, you can rely on action from General Crook, who is a man of great rectitude who was badly embarrassed by getting snatched from under the nose of his army, along with his intelligence officer who was supposed to prevent such things from happening.

"Do you understand your interest in keeping this from happening? Who knows, someone might even suggest that the lady's husband knew more than he let on. A really mean-spirited person might even suggest that Captain Michaelman and Captain McKenzie were seen riding at the back of the column during the abduction talking earnestly. It could even be noted that Captain Michaelman was not exchanged until after the war was ended and, hence, was still alive when better men were killed in the final struggle to restore our union.

"Perhaps, it would also interest you to know that Captain McKenzie is in Europe. He has married the woman whom you tried to hang as a spy. They are very happy. If anyone were to pursue her with a charge of espionage he would use every means at his disposal to see that such a person paid an extremely high price for that conduct.

"Do you follow my logic so far, Captain?"

Michaelman groaned and nodded his head.

"One final suggestion for your immediate action. You find a way to quash that warrant for Captain McKenzie. When you have done that successfully, it will be best for you to resign from the army and go back to your home in Ohio.

"We will be watching. Do not disappoint us. You are a very big target for all sorts of mischief, Captain."

Epilogue

"That was you in that buggy, wasn't it, Grandma?" the little boy asked, his eyes wide with excitement.

She smiled at the handsome child snuggled against her under the lap robe before the fire. "Yes, it was, Johnny."

"Were you scared when they caught you and then later when you were running away?" His faced was troubled at the thought of the danger.

"Yes, I was, but I knew that someone would come to help me."

"How did you know that?" he asked solemnly? "You never did get your Guard of Honor."

She paused for a long time and looked into the fire. The faces of Jack and George, the sergeant, 'Chilles, Scipio and Caesar, Bobby and Lon, Callista, the Yank, the tall cattle drover, Tom, and Tom Bennett and his strong and capable wife seemed to form in the flames. She turned and looked lovingly at the sleeping face of the old man across the fireplace from her and then said, "Oh, yes, I had the finest Guard of Honor that anyone can have—good, decent, brave men who watched over me and cared for me. And I hope that you will be one of my Guard of Honor too!"

Acknowledgments

I wish to thank all who have contributed to the writing of this book. I received incisive and valuable comments and corrections to the manuscript from Mr. Robert Goldich and Colonel Jim Kurtz. Bob, a retired manpower specialist and historian of broad knowledge, for The Congressional Research Service a friend of many years, helped greatly in balancing the characters and providing insightful criticism. Jim, a retired soldier of distinction, and expert on the American Civil War, combed out the errors in the military and historical part of the manuscript. It turned out that Jim had an Ohio Ancestor who ran into McNeil's Rangers during the Civil War.

The cover art features the painting *The Vedette*, Newell Conyers Wyeth, one of the foremost illustrators in our national history. The painting was first published in 1910 in Mary Johnston's novel, *Cease Firing*. In that publication, this superb, evocative painting was reproduced in half tone black and white. The reproduction did not do the painting justice, and Wyeth was understandably upset. The use of the painting for the cover was graciously authorized by Brandywine Museum, on behalf of the current owner. We hope that the quality of the reproduction and the prominence given to the work in this new story about Confederate cavalry soldiers would please Mr. Wyeth more than the original use of the painting.

The Author

Don Bowman grew up in the South in a family with direct connections to "The War," as it was called. His Texas family's service in the Civil War was extensive. His great-grandfather Bowman served in Company B of Gano's Squadron of Texas Cavalry along with Don's great-great uncle. Gano's Squadron served with Morgan's cavalry almost from the beginning of the Civil War. It became the basis of the 3rd Kentucky Cavalry (later re-designated the 7th Kentucky) when so many volunteers flocked to Morgan in Lexington that he had to organize a new regiment. Both men were captured and interned in Camp Douglas for twenty months at the end of Morgan's raid into the North in 1863. Exchanged in March of 1865, they are believed to have been part of the escort for Jefferson Davis during his flight from Richmond. Don heard stories of their service and captivity all of his life. Another great-grandfather served first in the 7th Texas Cavalry and later moved cattle from Texas across the Mississippi to supply the Confederacy with meat and leather. Another great-grandfather was a surgeon in Dick Taylor's army west of the Mississippi. A great-grandfather and another great-great uncle, his older brother on the Florida side of the family, also served in the cavalry and drove cattle north from Florida for the Confederacy. Their younger brother served in the 9th Georgia Infantry in Longstreet's Corps. He was captured during the fighting in The Wheat Field at Gettysburg.

An early interest in history planted by stories repeated by the children of these men blossomed when Don received an appointment to the United States Military Academy at West Point. After graduation, he served in the 82nd Airborne Division in the United States and in the Airborne Brigade of the 8th Infantry Division in Germany. In Korea, he served in the 1st Cavalry Division. After returning to West Point to serve on the staff, he rejoined the 1st Cavalry Division, now air cavalry, in Vietnam. During his service, Don commanded at every level from platoon to battalion and served on staffs at all levels from battalion to Department of the Army. During his career he taught at the Airborne School and the Ranger School where he was the deputy director. By the end of his active duty career, he had been awarded the Silver Star, the Legion of Merit, the Distinguished Flying Cross, the Bronze Star Medal with V device, and the Purple Heart. He holds the Combat Infantryman Badge, the Expert Infantryman Badge, the Ranger Tab, the Master Parachutist Badge, the Pathfinder Badge, the Army General Staff Badge, and the Army Recruiter's Badge. He is currently the treasurer of the National Ranger Memorial Foundation, Inc., and is a certified public accountant in public practice in Columbus, Georgia.

He has published articles in service journals and contributed to *Infantry Magazine* an article comparing his great-grandfather's service with Morgan's cavalry to his own service in the 1st Air Cavalry Division in Vietnam. This is his first full-length book. He began it while undergoing chemotherapy for cancer. The story took his mind off the treatment and gave him something to do during times of enforced inactivity. It was originally intended as a short story, but it took on a life of its own as the characters took over and began to do things that he had not planned for them to do. A life-long admirer of the writing of Colonel John W. Thomason, Jr., a fellow Texan and career marine, Don thought it was time for another story like those written by Thomason in the 1920s, '30s, and '40s.

Is the book biographical? Well, not exactly. The major events are historical. The interaction of historical characters with the fictional characters is invented, but the course of history followed much as it is described in the book. Are the fictional characters real people? They exhibit the characteristics of many people and are to some extent composites of real people mixed with invented characteristics. Strangely, they became real people as the book developed. Who would not like to know Cynthia Montgomery and John McKenzie?

LaVergne, TN USA
02 December 2010
207150LV00001B/1/P